BECOMING THE LUNA QUEEN

PREGNANT WITH FOUR ALPHAS' BABIES

BOOK SEVEN

BELLA MOONDRAGON
OLIVIA BHELLE KILDARE

For Rosaline and Ethan

CONTENTS

CHAPTER 1: A BETA'S DEATH

Adam

The massive gray wolf is right in front of me now, and in these seconds as I run toward them, a lifetime of emotion flashes in front of me.

Alpha Tristan has given me the go-ahead to take him down. Now, all I have to do is leap in and take him out.

Alastor's minions have backed away, and his clear focus is on the truly intimidating Alpha in front of him. He doesn't even sense me coming.

But all my senses are as sharp as steel, taking in a thousand mental pictures of my surroundings through scent, touch, sight, and even that basic-level sense I call instinct, which now readies my body to fight.

The scent of the pine trees is sharp and clear, as is the metallic smell of blood from the battle around me. Other scents from forest life are still faint, but the wild animals have left this place, probably at the onset of the battle.

I feel my muscles alternate from tense to relaxed as my paws rhythmically beat against the soft forest floor. My heart beats hard and steady, pumping the blood and adrenaline throughout my veins.

My mind steadies as I home in on my target, and I allow all my anger, hate, and rage at this man who has taken away my birthright flow through my body. My mind and body become one with this attack.

In the final seconds before my front paws leap off the ground, several things happen.

I feel an overwhelming warmth that I can only describe as coating my brain with a tingling sensation. In that instant, I feel more powerful, as though nothing could stop me. I know this to be the support of my beautiful mate, Shelby, who watches from a short distance, her soft chocolate fur standing on end in anticipation as she silently cheers me on.

The huge gray wolf in front of me turns his head toward me in that last second, and his eyes go wide, flashing with the realization that he has made a grave miscalculation in both sending away his guards and underestimating this cohesive, disciplined army of friends. Hatred and desperation come next to his eyes as he tries to turn and brace for the blow, but his arrogance has left him no time to defend himself.

I fly at him, claws extended and jaw wide open, aiming for his jugular. Right before I strike, I catch one last glimpse of his right eye, and in it I see... acceptance.

The blood flows over my teeth, its distinct coppery taste flooding over my tongue. Alastor loses his footing and stumbles back, and I go with him, landing on top of him, my teeth pushing one last piercing slice into his neck as his life fades away.

The forest goes silent and still as the rest of Alastor's wolves sense his death and stop fighting, some taking fatal blows as they reel in shock from their leader's death, others backing off in surrender and gratitude that the evil bastard is finally done with.

This one... was all mine.

~

KELLY

It all happens so fast.

Huge guards burst through the partially open steel door, half in wolf form and half in human form. Instinctively, I reach out my arms and pull in the two girls, bringing their heads in defensively against me and using my hands as protective shields.

The guards make quick work of us, one by one ripping the girls out of my arms and throwing them up against the wall. Each one screams as she is grabbed roughly by one of the human form guards, who quickly bind their wrists and ankles to the wall while their wails of pain fade into tears.

I am so upset by their plight that I barely feel my own body slamming up against the wall, and I am quickly restrained in the same way.

The guard in human form who is handling me moves his face in close. I can smell his stale, putrid breath against my neck. I look him straight and steady in the eye, and he smiles with filthy, crooked teeth as his disgusting eyes lower to look at my body.

As he starts to reach out his hand, another shifter quickly snaps at him. "That's enough," he says.

Instantly the creepy shifter backs up. His smile fades for a second but comes back again as he looks at me and slowly takes backward steps.

"Now," says the guy in charge. "It seems we have a little problem... with the help." For the last phrase, he turns his gaze toward Kara, who closes her eyes in a wince and tilts her head to the ground. But he's back looking at me in an instant. "Do I need to get graphic about what will happen the next time any of you act up?"

I shake my head but say nothing.

He nods. "Good," he says. "I'm sure you understand the ramifications of leaving employees such as Randolph here," he adds as he nods toward the creepy guard, "in charge of young ladies."

The look he gives to the girls then sends shivers up my spine. "Understood," I say simply. I figure the less I say right now, the better.

"Excellent," he says. "I think we've been a bit generous with food and water as well. I think we'll slow that up a bit now until you all learn to behave."

I nod. It's not like I have a choice with my arms chained above my head again, this time a bit tighter.

Without another word, he nods toward the other guards, who pile out the door. The clank of the steel door's lock sounds a lot more permanent now.

"Kelly?" asks Heather after a few minutes. "We ever git'n outta here?"

"Of course we are," I say. Right now, I'm not allowing myself to second-guess that answer. I have to believe that we'll survive and that Eli is on his way to rescue us right now.

I turned my attention to Kara, who is quietly weeping in the corner. I wish I could reach out to her, and anger flashes through my veins as I try in vain to break the chains off me.

"You're going to be okay," I tell her. "I have lots of people out looking for us, and I promise you, they'll find me. And when they find me, we're taking you along."

"But how will they find you?" she asks. "I don't even remember where we are. It's been so long...."

"Don't worry about it," I say. "My brother is a powerful Alpha, and he has a strong alliance with three other powerful Alphas. One of them is going to be the new Alpha King, so I promise you that when they come and rescue us, these people will pay for what they've done to us, and what they've done to you."

It's too dark now with the door shut to see her, but with my wolf's senses, I can make out her shadow against the wall to my right. I feel her let a breath out, and my heart breaks as she seems to be resigned to our fate.

"But they need to hurry," she says. "Mr. Donovan said they won't feed us for a while. That means he'll give all the food and water to the guards, and we get nothing. How will we last here with no one feeding us?"

She has a point, and it's very difficult to keep up my positive energy for her. Eventually, we could starve to death, or we could die from dehydration if they don't at least give us some sips of water once in a while. The thought of that creepy guard coming down here and getting close to the girls makes me sick to my stomach, but if we have to endure his proximity to get them some food and water, then we really have no choice.

"I just know it's going to be okay," I say. "I promise you, I have a lot of people out looking for me. Eventually, there's going to be some clue about where we've gone. If anyone can find me, it's my brother. He's strong and smart and tenacious. He won't give up until he finds me, and that means he'll find you, too."

I can feel her nod in the darkness. I relax against the wall and see if I can slide down into a sitting position. Miraculously, it's actually possible, and I don't even have my hands tied in an awkward, uncomfortable position anymore. The handcuff fasteners themselves are much tighter, but these chains seem longer somehow.

"We're going to be okay," I tell Kara and Heather.

And I just have to believe that it's true.

CHAPTER 2: THEY'RE GONE

Rose

It's almost dark outside when I open my eyes. I vaguely remember falling asleep, but it seems like it was much earlier in the day when I did that, so I'm astonished that none of the babies have woken me up.

Yawning, I sit up and note that the sounds coming from outside are not nearly as loud now as they were before either, and I have to wonder if the battle is over.

It seems crazy that I could fall asleep with a war raging on outside of my window and four babies sleeping in my room, but giving birth and then taking care of four babies, even with help, is exhausting. I'm so lucky to have help, like the healers and nurses from Mark's pack.

And Retta. She's been unexpectedly helpful.

Sitting up, I look at the closest bassinet, Trisha's, and see that my baby isn't in there. I think that's strange, and a little alarm goes off in my head, but I remind myself that someone probably just took her to change her diaper or rock her.

But then my eyes go to the next bassinet, which belongs to Reeva... and my other daughter isn't here either.

The alarm bells in the back of my head are frantic now as I look to see neither of my sons is here. I throw the blankets off of my legs and practically leap out of bed. "Retta?" I call, both with my mouth and in my head, using the mind-link. "Where are the babies?"

"Oh, are you awake?" she says back in my head quickly enough. "Don't worry! I just moved them to another room in the castle so that you could rest. I'll bring them back in just a minute."

"Where are they?" I'm already walking out into the hallway to the room where the babies were kept before. I notice there are no guards in the hallway now like there have been since the war started. I know that Mark told some guards to stay there and not move until he came back. I spin around a few times and see no one.

Walking into the old nursery, I see that there's no one here either.

And Retta isn't answering me very quickly.

"Retta? Where are you? Where are my kids? And do you know where the guards are?"

Again, the mind-link is silent. I continue to walk down the hallway, opening the doors that are unlocked and wishing I had a key for the ones that weren't, but when I knock, no one answers.

Then, I come to a door a few down from mine and notice something red on the floor, just a tinge of it, red liquid that seems to be coming from inside this room.

The hair on the back of my neck stands up as I recognize it as blood. All of the horrible possibilities flash through my mind, like, what if this is the blood of one of my babies currently flowing toward my bare toes?

As Retta says, "Stop panicking, Rose. We're on the second floor in one of the spare bedrooms."

I try the handle of the door. It's locked, but I refuse to stand here knowing blood is flowing out of this room and do nothing. I pull a bobby pin from my hair and twist it into the lock. Luckily for me, it opens.

What I see is possibly the most revolting sight I've ever had my eyes settle upon.

Bodies. Six of them. All male, all but one of them wearing the uniforms from Mark's guards.

All of them have had their throats ripped out, and their eyes are open in wide, horrified, terrifying looks.

I cover my mouth with both of my hands, to keep from screaming but also to keep from puking.

Are these the guards that were stationed outside of my door?

"Retta! Tell me where the fuck you are right now!" I demand, backing up against the wall behind me.

She is silent, and I know why.

I never should have trusted that bitch! I should have known that she was here to hurt me and my babies.

"Retta!" I scream in my head and with my mouth, as I spin around and run back to my room. I get dressed as quickly as I can, putting on shoes so that if I step in anything, at least it won't get on me.

Rushing back into the hallway, I yell, "Help! Everyone, help! The babies are missing and the guards are dead!"

I run down the hallway, still shouting, and Retta still has said nothing.

One of the nurses practically runs into me. "What did you say?" she asks, her eyes wide. She momentarily realizes how she's addressed me and starts to apologize, but I wave that off.

"No, there's no time! Start looking for my babies, now."

She nods and starts looking, but I don't think they are still in the castle.

I see one of Mark's higher-ups coming toward me in a rush. "The guards are in a room down by mine. You'll see–" Before I can finish the sentence, a shrill scream hits my ears. "Follow that noise."

I rush off, heading for the stairs, thinking I at least need to check to see if what Retta said was true, even though I'm certain it's not. Every person I run into wants to know how they can help, so I tell them to start looking for the babies.

But even before I reach the rooms on the second floor and start checking them, along with a maid who has a master key, I know in my heart my children aren't here, and it's taking every ounce of my energy to keep from losing my fucking mind!

When we reach the very last room and there are no babies, I want to crumple on the floor and cry.

But that's not the kind of mother I am. I will find my children. I will bring them back, and when I do… Retta and whoever the fuck she is working for will pay.

In my head, I call out to the Alphas, all four of them, even Eli, who is probably almost out of my range. "Guys, I don't care what you're doing or where you are, but you need to get back here right now!"

It's Mark who answers first. "What's wrong?"

I don't even know if I can form the words without breaking down. I had one job… and I failed. I failed my Alphas, I failed my babies, and I failed myself.

All I can say is, "She took them."

CHAPTER 3: WHO TOOK THE PUPS?

Reece

There's a lull in the fighting as everyone who is loyal to Alastor is finished off and the rest have surrendered, then I hear the panicked voice of my love wailing in my mind.

The three of us Alphas look at each other and instantly, I know that Tristan and Mark are thinking the same thing.

'Darlin'?' I ask in the mind-link. 'Are you saying—'

'I'm saying the babies are gone, and she took them!' Rose screams.

Still in wolf form from battle, we all tear away from our warriors and run toward Mark's castle. I don't think any of us even send word to our troops, but they must know that if we all run off like this, it's because Rose is in trouble. They can handle the surrendering warriors that used to belong to Alpha King Gene's battalions.

My heart feels like a rock and the knot in my stomach makes me want to vomit, but I don't. I just keep running faster. My mind can't work out who 'she' is right now, but that's not important. Someone has taken my daughter and the rest of Rose's babies, and whoever it is, that person is as good as dead right now.

After a few seconds of running, I can't feel my heartbeat, or my muscles, or anything in my body. I thank the Goddess that it's all moving by instinct now because I need to get to Rose as fast as I can. The rest of me is just... numb. And I know the other Alphas are feeling the same way.

It seems like forever before we reach the castle entrance, and all the guards split apart to give us a wide path; no doubt Mark has sent word ahead. I'm impressed that he can hold his mind together so well in this crisis. I know I can barely think straight.

'Where are you, little flower?' I hear Tristan call in the mind-link, which he's opened for all of us to hear. It's easier if we're all on the same page instantly rather than talking to Rose and then relaying it to the other Alphas. I guess his mind is sharp in crisis mode as well.

'Second floor,' she answers him, 'by the... I don't know. You'll see me.'

And we do. As soon as we fly up the grand staircase, there she is in the hallway, running from room to room slamming open doors. Only now I take it all in; the whole castle is abuzz with servants and other pack members everywhere doing the same thing—frantically looking for our pups.

We all shift back to human form and just as instantly, people are there with sweatpants for us. Tristan is the first to embrace Rose, and tears stream out of her eyes. But instead of looking hopeless and upset, there's a strong, determined look in her eyes. My Rose is now a mother, and nothing comes between a wolf mother and her pups.

"Darlin'," I say as I pull her in tight, holding her firmly but securely against me. There's no time for a kiss or any more affection because I hear the updates Mark's pack members are reporting to him behind me.

And this looks bad—very bad.

No one can find the babies, and there's a pile of dead guards down the hall from the room that not long ago was a nursery for my little girl and her brothers and sister. I hear the reports of all the blood and cringe at the news that Rose had been the one to discover it.

"Darlin'?" I say. "Are you sure it's okay for you to be running around like this?"

She pushes me back and instantly shoots me a look that makes me regret the question. Of course, she's not going to just lay there while others look for our pups, but I am worried that it's too soon to be up and around like this after giving birth to four pups at once.

She seems to realize this as her look softens. "I can't just lay there," she says, repeating my thoughts as though she'd heard them aloud. "Reece, my babies! Our babies!" It's now that the tears flow freely from her eyes, and I pull her in again tightly.

"We're going to find them," I say. "We will find them. Who took them?"

"That bitch Retta!" she says. "I knew I shouldn't have trusted her."

"I'm so sorry," says Mark. "I should have never—"

"That doesn't matter right now," says Tristan, interrupting him. "We have to focus on the search."

"Right," says Mark. "Tell us what happened, baby."

"I… I was asleep," says Rose. "I woke up and the babies were gone. She answered me in the mind-link… Retta… for a few minutes, and then silence. She said she was in a room up here, but she wasn't."

"Okay, darlin'," I say. "That means she was still nearby. Then she either went out of range or just stopped answering you on purpose."

"I've got scouts following tracks they just found," says Mark, "out back."

"Go!" screams Rose, and she starts to run with us.

Tristan holds her by her arms to stop her. "Little pearl, I'm sure you need to stay here."

"I'm not staying here when my babies are in danger!" she says, practically screaming.

"Miss Rose," says a nurse who's standing nearby. "You're going to need to constantly pump without the babies here, and we need to be by proper storage and a proper way to sterilize the equipment."

"She's right," Tristan says, running his hand over her cheek. "Little pearl, you know that the other Alphas and I are going to do everything in our power—and beyond—to find those pups and bring them back to you. We need you to be ready to feed them, and we need you to be healthy to care for them when they get back."

13

The look on her face breaks my heart. I know she wants to go looking for the pups every bit as much as we do, but Tristan is right.

"We'll find them," I say. "I promise."

She nods, her expression a mix of fear and sadness that makes that lump in my stomach grow. I squeeze her hand one last time before the other Alphas and I shift again and run toward the back of the castle.

We will find them.

Eli

"What is it?" asks Brent. He's driving, and we've been following a trail that had some fresh-looking tire tracks off the main highway. Luckily, it's a dirt road, so the tracks are still plainly visible.

But suddenly, I'm not feeling so well. It's the strangest thing I've ever felt. It's like some sort of a seed has hatched right in my stomach and is growing, but it's not really a seed, it's more like a rock, and it's getting heavier and heavier very quickly.

At the same time, my heartbeat feels strange. It's beating out of rhythm and feels like it's going to tear out of my chest. I double over from the pain and Brent pulls the SUV over and stops.

"Alpha?" he asks. "What is it?"

"I... I don't know," I say. "All of a sudden I'm sick."

"Did you eat something?" he asks, and I can see the worried look on his face.

Two other warriors are in the backseat, and they also express concern.

I shake my head. "I'll be fine," I say. "I just need a minute."

"Alpha," says Seline, one of the warriors. "I think you need to contact your mate."

"What?" I ask. I'm not sure what being sick to my stomach has to do with Rose.

"What you're feeling could be your mate in distress," she explains. "Please, try to reach her."

I'm horrified at the thought that something could be wrong with

Rose, so I try to reach her through the mind-link. We're pretty far away from Mark's castle, though, and I think I'm out of range because I get no answer.

I'd better be out of range.

"She's not answering," I say. "But I think we're out of range. Why do you think this has something to do with my mate?"

"Because, Alpha," she says, "I have had the same thing happen to me while my mate was in battle. He was gravely injured, and I was at home, but I felt his pain the moment it occurred."

This has me even more panicked about what might be happening to Rose right now. But the road I'm on… it could possibly lead to Kelly, and she's somewhere waiting to be rescued as well.

My heart tears in half trying to choose which path to pursue. If I make Brent turn around, that's like giving up on Kelly. But if Rose's in danger, that means the pups are in danger as well. I have to try to be there for them.

"Go," says Brent. "We'll go ahead on this path and keep looking for Kelly. But a feeling that strong… you need to pursue it and see what's happening with your mate. I'll have Sean meet you at the highway to drive you back. You'll get there faster."

I nod, already opening the door. Within seconds, I've shifted and am running back down the dirt road we've been exploring toward the main highway, trusting Brent to have my ride ready for me.

I have no idea what's wrong with Rose, but nothing will keep me from her side.

CHAPTER 4: KILL THE PUPS

RETTA

These babies are remarkably quiet as I lug them through the forest. It's almost as if they don't even mind that I'm stealing them away from their parents, from their home, from everything they've ever known.

Not that they know much of anything. They are tiny babies, after all, only a few days old, and I seriously doubt they know much about who their mother is, where they've been, or much else.

But in a way, I feel bad about this….

Not the kind of bad that's going to make me turn around and stomp my way back to the castle, but bad nevertheless.

After all, Rose is not who I thought she was.

I suppose I am exactly who she thought I was—stuck-up, manipulative, bitchy as hell. Yes, all of those words seem to describe me pretty well, even though I've been pretending to be something else the last few days.

I knew she would fall for it, though. Even though I always thought she was under the impression she was better than me and the other kids at school because her parents were our pack leaders, and apparently I was incorrect about that, I've always seen her as trusting and naive.

17

BELLA MOONDRAGON & OLIVIA BHELLE KILDARE

As I wander through the forest as fast as I can go with two babies strapped to my back and two babies strapped to my front, I think about all of the times in high school when we invited her to parties and other social gatherings. We had hoped she'd show up so we could pull pranks on her, but she never even came.

After speaking with her the last couple of days, I realize now that's because her parents wouldn't let her, not because she didn't want to. She wasn't allowed to do anything fun like that, and it turns out she spent a lot of her free time cleaning, working, and otherwise trying to appease her parents.

Of course, she's also a lot more intelligent than I realized. I suppose it's possible that Rose realized that if she had come to one of our parties we would've done something cruel to her.

I spent a lot of time in high school trying to come up with ways to put her in her place and punish her for being the Alpha's daughter without realizing she probably would've rather been anyone else in the world.

And none of those schemes ever came to fruition because she was too busy scrubbing toilets….

I can't think about any of that now. I'm not taking her children simply because I have despised her for most of my life. No, I'm taking her children because I've been paid handsomely to do so, and even though now I'm having second thoughts about all of this, I continue to rush through the woods even as I hear Rose's voice in my head.

I just hope she doesn't realize that if she has one of her Alphas command me to stop it will be a lot more difficult for me to do so. Their influence over me won't be as strong as my own Alpha's, but it would still make me hesitate.

Any amount of hesitation is a good way to get caught red handed. I can hardly believe I was able to slip out as easily as I was. When I told the other people caring for the babies to help me move them to another room silently, they had done so. When I told them that I would stay with the babies while they went to rest, they did so without hesitation, they were all so tired. And they believed that Rose and I were good friends, so I could be trusted.

When I'd slaughtered all of the guards in the hallway so they wouldn't see me taking the babies... well, I'd had help for that. I'd given a little treat to one of the guards and told him about all of the money "we" would be getting once we took the babies. I'd known the moment I looked at him that he was gullible. Once the others were dead, it was pretty easy to kill him.

I'd just bitten off his dongle, and then, when he started to bleed out, I'd slashed his throat. Easy as pie.

Killing isn't something I have no experience with. I've killed a lot of people since I left my home pack. It's the only way to survive in some places.

If my new employer hadn't tracked me down, I might still be in no-man's land, offering my services and killing those who don't want to pay fairly....

One of the babies starts to fuss, so I pick up speed, hoping to lull her back to sleep. It's the one with the curly black hair. I am really smitten with that one. I've never really liked babies before, but this one is so cute and has quite the personality. I can't remember her given name, but I know it starts with a T. I like J names better, so I've taken to calling her Jennifer.

I think... since my new boss wants to kill all of the babies anyway, I may ask if I can keep this one. I don't know if I'll raise her or sell her, but she's just got too big of a personality to be slaughtered....

I see a part in the trees ahead of me and know I'm almost to the road. I can hear Rose screaming and threatening me in my head now, but I press on, and then a car comes into view, and I smile because I'm almost home free.

'Retta! Stop right now!' a loud male voice says in my head, and my feet freeze in the grass a few feet from the car.

It's an Alpha, and I'm compelled to do as he says.

Of course, it doesn't always work on other packs, or else wars would be easily won by the loudest Alpha who would just tell all of the warriors on the other side to stop fighting...

"What are you doing?" my boss shouts from the car. "Get in here!"

My feet begin to move again. Not an Alpha, but close enough. I climb in, seeing there are no baby seats or anything. I can't lean back with these babies on my back.

"Help, please?"

From behind the steering wheel, there's a loud sigh, and then she takes the two boys off of my back and practically tosses them into the back seat. They wake up and start crying.

"Hey!" I shout. "You can't do that. They're just babies."

"Babies we are going to be killing in a few minutes." Her eyes are cold and dark.

I realize then that I don't want to kill any of the babies. They are just babies, after all. I have held them, rocked them, changed their diapers, and sang to them. None of them ever yelled at me, called me names, or otherwise did anything to offend me.

Babies are like dogs. So much better than real people....

She takes off driving so quickly, it's all I can do to keep the boys from falling. I manage to scoop them up and place them on my lap, shushing them, but the red-haired one is practically the same shade as his hair, he's so mad.

"What's the matter with you? Did you get attached?" my boss barks at me from the driver's seat of a stolen car that has the emblem of the crown on the door.

"No," I tell her, but that's not true. I stroke the black curly hair of the little girl I now call Jennifer. I am attached.

I don't want Rose to have her babies, but I don't want to kill them either.

The only problem is, I'm not in charge here, and I have very little influence over my new boss....

Luna Barbara.

CHAPTER 5: TRUE FRIENDSHIP

SHELBY

"Adam?" I ask as I watch the Alphas run off. I almost don't want to know what's going on because there's only one thing that could make those men move so quickly toward the castle.

I touch Adam's shoulder lightly, and he sets the warm palm of his hand over mine. In any other moment, that would be comforting, but right now, there's an ache growing in the pit of my stomach. This is about Rose or the pups, and I know it's bad news.

He nods and looks into my eyes. "The pups are missing," is all he needs to say.

I'm not a mother—I certainly hope to be one someday—but just those four words invoke an instant panic response that I feel throughout my body. I've never even had a chance to meet the little ones yet, but all I want to do is shift and run right behind the Alphas to help them find them right now.

That instinctive feeling subsides slowly while I consider the bigger picture. We've just finished up a bloody battle that has ended in the death of a rival Beta and the surrender of a good many warriors, and organizing that surrender is the task assigned to Adam right now. The best thing that he can do for those babies at the moment is to take care of things so that the Alphas don't have to worry about what's left of the battlefield.

Adam has obviously come to the same conclusion because he's now working closely with the other Betas—well, I guess technically Adam isn't a Beta any more, but still—the other Betas that belong to the four Alphas' packs to organize everyone that's left.

With their roles clear, it's time for me to go do my part.

"I have to go to Rose," I say.

Adam breaks off from the man he's speaking with and pulls me to the side. "Okay," he says. "But please be careful, my mate."

"I will," I say, stealing a quick kiss before shifting and running toward Alpha Mark's castle myself.

I know that the Alphas wouldn't ever let Rose go after the babies with them, not when it's been such a short time after she gave birth to the four pups. So that means she's alone—well, not alone since I'm sure all the nurses and servants are with her—but what she needs right now is a friend.

It takes a frighteningly short amount of time to arrive at the castle, considering that we just fought a brutal battle so close by. It seems that Adam has had a Beta inform the guards ahead of time because when I arrive here, they quickly let me in after I shift, get dressed, and I tell them my name. I find Rose upstairs where a maid has led me. Thankfully, she's laying down in her bed.

But she doesn't look well, not at all.

"Rose!" I say as I walk into her room.

When she sees me, she stands up instantly and draws me in for a hug. "Shelby!" she says. "That bitch... that bitch took my babies!"

"I know," I say. "Well, I know they're gone... but what bitch do you mean?"

"Retta," she says.

I shake my head and try to lead her back to her bed. She doesn't look well. "You can tell me in a minute," I say. "Please lay down while we talk."

"I'm so sick of everyone telling me to lay down!" she shouts, and it shocks me a little. "I'm sorry," she adds. "I know you're trying to help.

It's just that I can't stand the thought of my babies being missing... where they are, who's with them, whether they're okay..."

"Okay," I say, laying her down in her bed and taking her by both arms. "You need to breathe for me, hun. I can only imagine what you're going through."

She nods while she struggles to take a couple of deep breaths. "My Alphas... they're out there looking for them," she says.

"I know. And they're going to find them. They will move the Goddess' heaven and earth to get them back to you."

"I know," she says. "It's just so hard to sit here waiting."

"I know the four of them will come through," I say.

"Well, that's just it," she says. "Eli... he's not here."

"Where's Eli?"

"Looking for Kelly," she says. "Oh, Shelby! Kelly is missing, too!"

"Kelly took the babies?" I'm confused. Why would Kelly take her own nephew?

Rose shakes her head. "No, she was missing before," she says. "When Eli came back, he didn't bring Kelly with him."

"I'm going to need you to back up a little bit," I say. "Okay, I had heard that Eli was back. Just in time for the birth, right?"

Rose nods. "Yes, just in time for—Eli!!"

Rose's eyes light up, and I look in the direction of the door. It's Eli, so I back up a few steps to let him get through to Rose.

"My Goddess," Eli says. "Are you all right, baby?"

Their embrace is tight and desperate, and Rose seems to want him to pull her right out of the bed, but he gently lays her back down and runs his hand over her cheek.

Tears start pouring down her face as though she'd been holding back for hours. "Our little boy... the babies! Eli, I can't live without them!"

"I know, baby," he says, gently brushing the hair out of her eyes and finishing with his thumb wiping her tears. "I knew something was wrong, so I returned, and I was told what happened. I came to see you first, then I'm going to join the others out looking for them."

"Did you find Kelly?" she asks.

He shakes his head. "No, but some very good people are out looking for her," he says. "I felt you... I felt your pain and knew I had to come back."

"I needed you," she says, and the look in her eyes is pleading and hopeful, but tears are still flowing uncontrollably.

"I know, baby," he says. "And I need you to stay here while I go out looking with the others. Shelby can stay with you." He looks up to me and nods, and I nod back in understanding. "You need to be healthy for the babies once we bring them home."

"That's what the others keep saying," she says. "But Eli, I can't stand it! I just can't stand it!"

Her breathing gets more erratic now, and I move over to the other side of the bed. "Rose," I tell her. "You're going to have to try to relax." I look up at the nearest nurse and she nods in understanding. "We're going to get you something to calm you down."

"But the babies need my milk," she says, shaking her head.

"I'm sure that the herbs they bring will protect your milk," I say. I don't know that for sure, but these women nurses look experienced, so surely, they know what to give a breastfeeding woman who is having this kind of emotional trauma. My heart just aches for Rose and the babies.

Eli strokes her face once more and gives her a gentle kiss while the nurse hands Eli a jar of salve. "Alpha, putting that on her chest will help calm her," she says.

Alpha Eli carefully rubs some on her, and I can see immediate results as Rose's breathing starts to return to normal. The scent is pleasant, like lavender mixed with something I can't quite put my finger on.

"I have to go now, love," he says. "I've messaged the other Alphas, and I'll be joining them. You stay with Shelby, and please, be safe."

Rose nods, her eyelids closing gently as he squeezes her hand once more before kissing her lightly on the lips. He looks at me one last time with a nod and heads out the door.

She looks rested now, so I pull up a nearby chair, careful not to disturb her by letting the legs screech on the smooth floor. I have a lot of unanswered questions, and since Rose is drifting off into a restless sleep, I won't know the answers for a while now, so I settle in and get comfortable.

I never found out who this Retta is, but if she's evil enough to steal four new pups from Rose, I don't want to know her. And I don't want to know how the hell she was let within a mile of Rose and the pups if she's that kind of a person.

Whoever she is, that doesn't matter right now. I'm sure the four Alphas will team up to get these babies back quickly, hopefully before Rose wakes up next.

In the meantime, I'll be what she needs most right now—a true friend.

CHAPTER 6: I'VE BEEN CHEATED!

RETTA

Barbara hits a giant rut in the road, and all five of us, the four babies and I, get jolted out of our seat. I hit my head on the ceiling of the shitty SUV she's "borrowed" from King Gene.

It turns out the old king has paid her handsomely to steal and kill these babies. They are all screaming their little heads off, probably hungry, and while I did think to bring some of the pumped milk Rose had ready for them along for the ride, I can't possibly feed all four of them at the same time with Helen Keller behind the wheel.

"Will you please be more careful?" I shout at the Luna as I brace myself for another impact. The woman can't drive a car to save her fucking life!

"I am going fast to get away from those asshole Alphas. If you didn't know, they are chasing us." She turns to glare at me and only turns back to the road in time to barely avoid a large tree.

I screech. "Yes, but they're likely on foot! We have time!"

"No, we don't have time!" she screams at me. "We have to get away. I have their children, you fucking moron! They're huge, muscular Alphas who will rip me apart if they catch me—and not in a fun way."

"What's a fun way to be ripped apart?" I ask, confused, and when I see her face, a wicked smile spreading across it as she looks dreamily into the distance, I am sorry that I asked.

She clears her throat and doesn't answer, and I'm glad for that.

"The train station is right up here about three miles," she explains. "King Gene has a house about thirty miles down the tracks. We'll hop on a train, take these babies to his secluded dwelling, dispatch them there, and then, we'll be on the lam until we can get back to the castle. King Gene has promised to protect me at all costs once I execute this task–and the babies."

She's back to focusing on the road, but I am thinking long and hard about what she's just said. "He's promised to protect you?" I repeat.

"That's right," she says, nonchalantly. "As he should! This is dangerous work I'm doing."

I clear my throat, unable to hear it even myself over the sounds of all of the crying. "What about me?" I ask her.

"Oh, right. You. Well, I mean, I'm happy to have your help in keeping me safe, too. I just don't figure you'd be much help with that. And besides, I figure you'll be taking the money King Gene gave you and getting the hell out of here," she says with a simple shrug.

"King Gene didn't give me any money," I say, my voice squeaking a bit as I try to establish exactly what's going on here. "My deal is with you, not him."

"He didn't?" She's looking at me again and not the road, and my life flashes before my eyes as I point out the windshield at a giant rock in the road, unable to speak. She turns her attention back to it, just in time to avoid catastrophe. "Well, you'll have to take that up with him."

"But you're the one who contacted me and promised me payment!" I remind her, anger growing inside of me. She knows she promised to pay me. She's just acting dumb on purpose as a way to keep from having to give me the money she said she would. I could do a lot with fifty thousand gold coins!

"Listen, Reba," she begins.

"Retta!" I correct her.

"Right. Whatever. You're just a little cog in this operation. You have nothing to do with anything, so you should just be happy that I chose you to help with such an important assignment." She's talking like I'm supposed to be grateful I just double-crossed four powerful Alphas and stole their children all because I "get" to help her!

"Oh, hell no!" I shout at her. "If you think I'm going to continue to help you with this plan without getting paid, you can kiss my ass. At this point, even if you let me keep one of the babies as payment, I wouldn't accept. I want coins, and I want them now!"

"Keep one of the babies?" she laughs. "What in the world would make you think I'd ever consider that? Hell, no. These babies are dying. I wish I could kill them right now, but King Gene wants them killed ritualistically, as a sacrifice to the devil, so I can't just throw them out the window to make them shut the fuck up."

"You aren't even listening to a damn word I'm saying!" I shout at her. "I said I want my money!"

"And I said you'll have to take that up with King Gene!"

"No, I want it from you, and I want it now!"

She turns to hit me, her hand shifting into a wolf's paw with long claws as she takes a swing, and I raise my arm to block her. Just then, the car swerves, hitting another deep rut, and all I can see ahead of us are long, pine-needle-covered tree branches.

I scream louder than the babies when the front of the car rams into the trunk of a giant pine tree. Glass shatters, my head slams into the dashboard, but my instinct tells me to protect the babies, even though they are meant to die.

My airbag doesn't go off, and that's probably a good thing for the children because they would've been smashed. When the car has stopped, my head is spinning, throbbing, and the crying has all but stopped.

Are they dead?

I look down at the tiny babies still in my lap, and they are covered with little pieces of glass. A couple of them have bloody scratches on their faces and hands. but they are all still breathing, their eyes wide with fear.

Then... they break out into even louder cries of distress.

"It's okay, babies!" My head is still swimming, but I manage to get the glass off of them. None of them are hurt badly. That's a miracle.

My eyes go to Barbara, who is quiet for the first time. The Luna's face is buried in the airbag, and she's not moving.

Grabbing the back of her hair, I pull her face up and see that bruises are already starting to form, and a trickle of blood is pouring from her mouth.

She's out cold.

I can't help but chuckle.

I switch the car off, dig through her pockets and find a coin purse full of gold, then get out of the car, which is still smoking.

It won't be hard for the Alphas to find this. I need to hurry. And I need to ditch these babies as soon as I can. I head toward the village Barbara told me about, which isn't far now. Maybe I can find someone to take three of the babies there.

But not the little girl with the black curls. That one is mine.

I wonder what King Gene will do to Barbara when he finds out he didn't get his ritual....

CHAPTER 7: BLOOD IN THE WRECKAGE

Eli

Leaving Rose once again is heartbreaking, but knowing that my son—and the other pups—are out there with some crazy woman is just as unbearable. I'm thankful for Shelby because at least there's one very trusted friend who can be there with her while she waits for us to return with the pups.

And we will return with the pups—or die trying.

'Shelby's with Rose,' I tell the others in the mind-link as I race toward their location. I know that information will help put their minds at ease as well.

'We just took a southwest turn,' says Reece. 'The scent is getting stronger now. We're definitely on the right path.'

'I doubt I'll catch up with you, but keep giving updates, and I'm right behind you,' I say. I'm running at full speed in my wolf form, but the other Alphas are doing the same, and they have quite a head start on me.

'Stop!' says Mark.

I don't want to stop, but the way he says it makes me feel like it's the right choice, so I slow down a bit while he continues, 'We've hit a road, and there are tire tracks, so they're in a car. If you're not far and can head back for a vehicle, you can meet up with some of my warriors and cut them off.'

I nod, even though no one is around, while I make a complete U-turn and run top speed back to Mark's castle.

'I'll send word ahead to have vehicles and a team ready,' he says. 'We'll keep going in this direction.'

Luckily, I haven't been running long, so it's only about five minutes until I'm back at the castle, and as expected, Mark's pack is ready with a group of vehicles and a bunch of determined-looking warriors. I jump in still in wolf form, and an assistant hands me clothes from the backseat, which I change into as the driver takes off.

"Alpha Mark has given us directions," the driver says. "I know these roads well. If they're on Rural Road Five—that's the dirt road Alpha Mark found the tire tracks on—then it'll be easy to head them off if we go to Highway Seven."

I nod as I throw the shirt over my head and completely trust that this man knows where he's going. I've been to Mark's territory before, but it was a long time ago, and I certainly didn't memorize the roads.

'What's going on?' asks Rose in my mind.

I'd hoped she would sleep longer, but apparently not. She'd drifted off after I'd rubbed that herbal salve on her chest that the nurse had handed me, and it did seem to calm her quickly. I guess in her panicked state, the effects hadn't lasted long.

'I'm in a vehicle now,' I tell her. She certainly has every right to know exactly what's going on in the search for the pups—for my son and the others. 'The other Alphas found tire tracks on a road, so some warriors and I are looping around to get ahead of... whoever it is that has the babies.'

'Retta,' she says. And before I can ask, she continues, 'Retta is a part of my parents' pack, and I used to go to school with her. She was mean then but acted like she's nice now. She fooled us.... She fooled me into thinking that she was a different person now, that my parents had sent her to help with the pups. I knew I shouldn't have trusted her, but I just wanted to believe—"

'Baby, it's okay,' I say to her. 'You're a kind soul, and you want to believe the best in people. There's nothing wrong with that.'

'But it got our son stolen!' she says. 'It got all the pups kidnapped, and now they're with that bitch, and who knows who else?! Eli, she wouldn't have taken them if there wasn't something in it for her. Someone, somewhere has offered her money for our babies, or she wouldn't have done what she did. I just know that someone dangerous has them! Eli, who would it be?'

'I don't know, baby,' I say. 'But I promise we'll get all the babies back safe and sound, then we'll catch this Retta person, and whoever paid her, and lock them away forever.'

'After I get a piece of her,' she says.

'I know how you feel, baby,' I say. 'Let's just get the pups back safely first, and then we'll worry about that evil woman later. She's not important right now.'

'Eli, I—"

'I know, Rose,' I say. 'I know.' She doesn't have to finish that sentence. There's really no way to use words to explain this feeling we're all having right now anyway. Panic is a part of it, and anger, and rage. But none of those words really do justice to the feeling you get when your child is missing, and someone very evil has a hold of them.

It's a nightmare.

"Which way does this road lead?" I ask. I completely trust the driver, but I just feel like I need to get more information right now. In a situation where I have no control, I need as much information as I can get.

"It goes north for a bit before it meets up with Highway Seven," the driver says. He has an understanding tone in his voice. He knows how horrified I am right now, even though he can never completely under-stand. And he knows his Alpha is in the same state that I'm in right now. "From there, it makes a big loop before heading back in the direction of Rural Road Five. That gives us enough road that there's no way they could have passed us. We'll run right into them, with Alpha Mark and the others closing in on them from behind. We'll cut them off for sure."

"Thank you," I say. The assistant in the backseat hands me a bottle of water, which I happily accept. The other Alphas have been running for a long time. If I can keep up my strength and stay hydrated, I'll be in the best shape of all the Alphas to take on whatever is waiting for us when we cut off Retta and the pups. After all, if there was a car waiting, and that means she has help. If it's another Alpha, I'd better be ready to fight hard.

I have a few ideas about who that might be, but I'll wait and see for myself.

It felt like forever, but I'm sure it wasn't really that long before we reached the highway and started circling around to get back to the dirt road Retta had escaped on.

'Any news?' asks Rose in my mind.

'Nothing yet, baby,' I say. 'But we're getting closer. We had to drive around for a bit so we could be in a position to cut her off. As soon as I know anything, I will tell you, sweetie.'

'I know you will,' she says.

Eventually we reached a dirt road that slowed down our progress quite a bit as the driver worked to avoid as many potholes as he could.

'There's something up ahead,' Tristan tells me in my mind. I can tell that the message is only going to me and the other Alphas, so I'm very nervous about what he's found out there if he doesn't want to tell Rose.

'What is it?' I ask.

There's silence for a while, and I swear my heart isn't even beating. 'Tristan?'

'It's… it's a car wreck,' he says.

At that, a boulder drops in the pit of my stomach, and my heart freezes. So much flashed before my eyes—how I'd arrived just in time for little Ethan's birth, how I'd brushed back his little tufts of red hair while his little eyes looked up at me, how I'd sit and watch him sleep, how I'd watch Rose's beautiful face light up when she held our son.

I just can't… I cannot have lost him–not now. Not ever. My heart would rip into shreds.

Moments later, we round a corner and see the same scene up ahead that Tristan had described. The car looks crushed and for a moment, I can't even breathe.

'Tristan?' I say. 'What do you see?'

He doesn't have time to answer because I have already jumped out of the vehicle, before it even comes to a stop, and ran over to the wreckage. I stand there for a moment in about the same level of shock as the other Alphas as we assess the situation.

In the front seat is a woman that I quickly recognize as Barbara, slumped over and bleeding against a deployed airbag. The passenger side door is open, and the seat has what must be splotches of blood and broken glass all over the place. But it's empty... whoever had been there is clearly gone.

But there is one thing there that makes my stomach churn.

A blue, empty, baby blanket--covered in blood.

CHAPTER 8: HOW MUCH FOR THE BABIES?

Retta

I've got to get the fuck out of here!

I'm carrying four babies, limping through the forest, bleeding a bit from my leg and one of my arms, and I can feel the Alphas closing in.

The village is just up ahead, on the other side of these trees. From what I can tell, looking at the rooftops peeking through the tops of the trees, it's a pretty good-sized town. I'm hoping that means I might be able to unload a baby or two and get on a train out of here.

Selling babies in this day and age isn't as easy as it used to be. Back in the day, you could sell a baby for a couple of hundred gold coins, no questions asked. There was none of that, "Is it your baby? Where did you get it? Is it healthy? Why is it so ugly?" business I'm sure I'll encounter today. No, it's going to be a lot harder for me to sell these little brats than it would've been back in my grandmother's time.

Not that my grandmother was in the habit of selling royal babies, though I wouldn't put it past her. I'm not the first person in my family to have scrupulous morals.

At least the little fuckers have stopped screaming now. The other little girl has a set of lungs on her like a banshee in heat, and I do everything I can to keep her quiet so that she doesn't wake up my baby–the one I'm going to keep.

I've been rethinking the name I've been calling her and decided to name her Astrid. I think it has an ethereal quality to it. Perhaps she will be closer to the Moon Goddess because of her doting mother's forethought.

I pass a farmhouse on the outskirts of the village and see an older couple working in a garden outside of their house. Immediately, their eyes are on me, and I sense unease washing over them as their questioning glances smolder.

"Good day," I call to them. "Just… taking the kids for a walk."

"Why you got all them babies?" the man calls to me.

"Oh, I'm a nanny," I say. "For an important woman in the village."

"Why you got blood on your dress?" the woman asks me. "You okay?"

"I'm fine. Just… scratched my arm on a tree trying to keep the babies happy." One of them whimpers a bit, and I almost shout at him to shut his fucking mouth, but I remember I'm being watched.

"What's the name of your lady?" The old woman looks like she's not sure about my story. I need to get away from here.

"Uhm… Bar–dia. Bardia. Bardia Livingstone. Now, if you'll excuse me…." I hurry past them and hear the man ask his wife if she knows who that is.

"I ain't never heard of such a person, and I've lived here my whole life," she says.

I don't even turn around. I'm sure they're using the mind-link right now to contact the guards in the village, who are probably under Alpha Mark's authority. If they see me, they'll know what I've done as I'm certain that the Alphas have alerted all of the authorities about a woman carrying four babies.

I suddenly realize I look very suspicious carrying all of these babies.

A change in plans is in order. Quickly, I scour the surrounding area and see an old falling-down structure in the distance. When I get to it, I see it's uninhabitable, with holes in the ceiling and plants growing all through it, but it looks like it used to be a cabin.

This will have to do.

I unstrap three of the babies, only keeping the loud girl with me. "Sorry, kids," I say. "I'll be back. I hope nothing eats you while I'm gone. If something does, I'll be missing out on a lot of money."

With that, I take off to the village carrying Screamy, listening to the other babies begin to fuss as I disappear.

My feet tell me to head for the seedier part of town. No sense in going to a ritzy part to sell a baby. I walk around for a little while until I see a red lit-up sign that says, "Roxy's Place." I'm not about to try to sell a baby at a brothel because whores don't need any extra babies, but this tells me I'm in the right place.

With the little girl subdued for now, I go into a bar and approach the bartender.

He's probably about my dad's age and looks agitated as hell. "You can't bring a baby in a bar!" he snaps at me.

"I know that," I tell him, forcing a smile. "Listen, I was hoping you could help me out." I give him a seductive glance, but his eyes go to my bloody arms. I grab some napkins off of the counter and wipe off the red streaks.

"What do you want?" he asks.

"Do you know anyone who might be interested in… taking this kid from me?" I look down at the sleeping princess, and think of all of the money she's really worth.

"You're trying to sell your kid?" he asks for clarification.

Shrugging, I say, "I'm trying to sell A kid."

He chuckles under his breath. "Yeah, I know someone who might be interested, but she probably won't fetch that much. She anyone special?"

Not knowing if I can trust the barkeep, I say. "Maybe."

The look he gives me next isn't very approving, but he picks up the phone and dials a number. "Stevie?" he asks. "Hey, it's Pat. I got some lady here who wants to sell a baby." There's a little bit of discussion before he finally says. "Got it." He hangs up the phone and says, "He'll be right down."

"Thanks," I tell him and sink onto a barstool. I have no fucking idea what time it is, but I figure it's gotta be five o'clock somewhere. I have some money I stole from Rose and other people in the castle so I say, "Can I have a scotch on the rocks, please?"

The bartender pours my drink, and I down it before ordering another. I'm still sipping on the second one when I feel a presence over my left shoulder. I turn back to look at the door and see a tall, thin, unassuming looking man standing there.

"Hey, Steve-O," the barkeeper says, waving him over.

"This is the guy who wants to buy this baby?" I ask. He looks like a computer geek, not a criminal.

But when he smiles, I see there's a lot more to him than meets the eye. An evil gleam glimmers in his dark orbs, his teeth are sharp, and his voice is gravelly. "How many babies you got to sell?"

CHAPTER 9: I'M GOING TO BRING THEM HOME!

TRISTAN

I'm horrified—but looking up at the faces of the two Alphas who have baby boys—Eli and Mark—I see a whole new level of nightmare in their eyes.

The baby blanket left behind is blue, one that was embroidered by Mark's pack members exclusively for Rose's pups. Some very sweet older ladies had given us a gift of several pink and blue blankets for the newborns, so we'd always have plenty, and the look on Rose's face when she handled the soft, warm fabric is something I'll never forget.

But now… now one of those same blankets is lying on the floor of the front seat of this car, covered in dangerous-looking shards of broken glass—and drops of blood. Eli and Mark look like they're somewhere between throwing up and wanting to tear whoever did this to shreds.

I'm not far from that feeling myself, since clearly all the pups were in this car and now, we have no idea where they are. My little Trisha is missing… she's somewhere, and the person who has her right now is very evil indeed.

But it's not the driver of this car, who is slumped over the steering wheel moaning. I snap out of my horror just long enough to notice

41

that this car is very familiar. It has come from Gene's fleet of cars from the royal garage of Black Rock, the cars I've often used myself for various trips out of the castle since I'd begun staying there for that stupid competition. Well, it wasn't stupid in the sense that I got to meet Rose, which probably would have been impossible before, but the last thing on my mind right now was being the next Alpha King.

No, right now, I want to drag whoever it is moaning in the front seat of this car out by her hair. Yes, it's a woman, and something about her is way too familiar.

By now, Eli has stepped forward and grabbed the blanket, and after he shakes off the broken glass and takes a whiff of the pup's scent who'd used to be wrapped up in it, I know for sure that I never want to be on the receiving line of the kind of anger that's seething inside him right now.

I step around him to the front and yank the woman's head back. The airbag had deployed, and it was half-deflated in front of her, but that hadn't kept the glass from cutting up her face.

And boy, do I know that face.

As I pull her out of the car, she's helping out at first, pulling herself to her feet.

"Barbara," I say in a voice that doesn't even sound like me.

She coughs, and her eyes go wide, then she instantly goes limp as though her legs have suddenly failed her. "I... I can't... move," she says in an obviously fake faint voice.

I let go and drop her to the ground, but she suddenly finds the strength and rights herself, standing up. She stares at us all for a moment and then says, "Thank the Goddess you're here!"

"What?!" I ask, being in no mood for her crap.

She seems to relax a bit as if she'd worked out the story in her head and thinks she can pull it off.

"You're here!" she says. "I caught the kidnapper red-handed, some bitch girl. And I was taking her... taking her back with the babies when she hit me and caused me to lose control of the car. Yes, that's what happened... I mean, she's escaped!"

"We all know that's bullshit, Barbara," says Reece. "Which way did she fucking go? You'd better talk quick before I let one of these guys tear you to shreds." He points his thumb back toward Eli and Mark, who both still have looks on their faces that I can't even describe, looks that make Barbara's eyes go wide again with the deepest level of fear I've ever seen.

"I-I don't know," she says. "She hit me! And it made me wreck the car while she escaped!"

Eli made a move toward her, and I said, "I strongly suggest you drop the crap, Barbara. You're just barely alive right now, and I'd highly recommend that you don't piss us off for one millisecond longer than you already have."

"Okay… okay," she says. "Just don't kill me."

"No promises," says Eli in a low, guttural voice that I didn't even recognize as his. "Which way?" He's using his Alpha tone, and it works easily on Barbara. I'm surprised he's in a state of mind where he can engage his Alpha voice.

"I… I didn't see much," she says, suddenly very cooperative. "But I remember hearing the babies cry over to the right."

I shudder at the description. The children were crying…. How long had they been without food? Was that Retta person hurting them? She didn't have her own pups, so she surely couldn't nurse them, and since she's a kidnapper, she certainly can't care for them. Time is ticking away on their safety.

Evidently, Eli feels the same way because, with a single nod, he starts running off in the direction Barbara had indicated, with Mark and Reece close on his heels.

I'm not going to waste time dealing with Barbara. I bark out some quick instructions to Mark's warriors, who know instinctively that their own Alpha's words would have been the same, ordering them to throw Barbara into Mark's dungeon until we figure out what to do with her.

I hear Barbara's pleading cries and fake moans of pain disappear into the background as I shift and follow Eli and the other Alphas.

We have to find our children, and fast.

~

ROSE

"They're not answering me," I say. "Shelby, why wouldn't they answer me?!" I'm starting to panic, and it's hard to catch my breath.

"Rose, I'm sure it's nothing," Shelby says, trying to calm me down.

I'm pacing around the room now, and any attempts to keep me lying in that bed are definitely useless at this point. I know everyone wants me to take care of myself and be healthy when the babies return, but what difference does it make right now?

There is no nightmare worse than having your children missing and in the hands of some horrible people. Nothing worse except... and I'm not going there. No, I am most definitely not going to go there. My Alphas would never let anything that terrible happen.

I reach out to them again, this time calling for Tristan. Maybe he'll have some answers for me. Not knowing is the worst part... well, almost the worst part.

'Little flower,' he says. 'We're getting closer. Please, please try to relax. Just work on getting enough milk ready for the pups when we bring them home.'

Tears come to my eyes. I'm so worried about finding them, about whether they're okay, whether anyone has physically harmed them, and it's been at least an hour since I thought about how they haven't eaten lately. I thought about it when I was pumping, but that had been so long ago. What kind of mother am I?! My babies are off somewhere starving, and I'm just sitting here doing absolutely nothing to help them!

"Rose?"

I barely hear Shelby's voice as I'm walking out of my room.

"Rose!" she says, getting louder as I move farther down the hall. "Rose! Please come back!"

"I can't!" I scream. "I have to do something! I can't just sit here pacing around a room when my babies are starving!"

I hear Shelby's footsteps running after me, and there are a few nurses also running after me, and I can hear them frantically grabbing

44

supplies as they break into a run. If the whole damn castle is going to follow me to rescue my babies, then so be it. But I'm sure as hell not waiting here for one second longer while my innocent babies need me.

As I head out of the castle, I run straight into Adam.

"Rose," he says. "Please, it's too dangerous out there." No doubt Shelby had mind-linked with him to stop me at the front gate.

"Dangerous… dangerous is exactly why I'm going!" I scream at him. "My pups, my innocent babies, are out there where it's dangerous, and I'm going to help bring them home!"

I can see by the look in his eyes that he knows it's hopeless to try to stop me. By now, Shelby has caught up with me as well.

"If you're going," she says, "we're going with you. Just give me five minutes to let these ladies put together some proper supplies for you. Please, Rose. Just five minutes."

I look into her eyes, and I can see my friend is with me now in this, so I nod, and she calls out lots of orders as the nurses and servants gather backpacks full of supplies for pumping and for just general traveling. It's much sooner than five minutes before everything is ready, so I throw on a backpack and head out the door with Shelby and Adam by my side and a bunch of warriors backing us up.

I open the mind-link to all four of my Alphas.

'Where are you?' I ask.

CHAPTER 10: I SHOULD HAVE SOLD THEM ALL

Retta

In a seedy bar, in a village I've never been in before, I'm approached by a questionable looking man who wants to know if this baby I've got strapped to my chest is the only one I have to sell.

"What do you mean?" I ask him. "Do I look like I just had a fucking litter of pups?"

He chuckles under his breath. "No, gorgeous. You don't look like you just gave birth to a damn pup at all. I'm just asking because I kind of got the impression that one isn't yours. Maybe you got some sort of a baby trafficking ring going on?"

It's an interesting question. I should probably tell him no, that this is the only baby I have, and it's mine, that I gave birth to the pup myself, and the reason I look so great is because I have fabulous genes.

but I know that the Alphas are going to be on to me soon, and I need to get rid of these brats as quickly as possible, so even though it might be more profitable for me to get rid of the kids one at a time, if he wants to offer me a price for all three, I'm down with that.

"I've got three," I tell him. "Two boys and one girl. You interested in all of 'em?"

"Maybe," he says. "Let me see that one."

I look down at the little girl. She's sleeping right now. It's the first time she's shut her damn mouth since the car wreck. I'm leery of moving her for fear she might start screeching again.

But I can't expect him to make an offer on a baby without examining it. Reluctantly, I unstrap her and hand her over to him. Immediately, she starts to whimper.

"Holy hell!" he says. "When was the last time you changed this kid's diaper? She's loaded!"

I hadn't noticed, honestly. I've been so nervous about getting the babies sold, it didn't even register that she'd shit herself.

With a frustrated sigh, I take a diaper out of the pack and plop her down on the bar.

"What the fuck you think you're doing?" the barkeep asks me. "You are not changing a shitty diaper in here! Go in the bathroom!"

I grumble again but lift her up and do what he says, going into the bathroom and changing her diaper.

Thankfully, I know how to do this now. There's no changing table since this is a bar, but I do see a counter by the sink, so I plop her down there and get her pants changed. He wasn't kidding–she was full all right. I imagine the other babies are probably needing changed, too.

She's also hungry. She's rooting around, trying to get her thumb in her mouth. Stupid baby thinks there might be milk in her own thumb.

I have some stuff to make a bottle, but I really don't want to screw with it right now. Instead, I just pick her up and take her back out to the man who wants to buy babies. Stevie, I think his name is. He sounds like a prick. He's probably the kind of guy who stabs his best friends in the back without even thinking twice, the kind of guy who takes a job at a company, throws a baby fit over something, and then sues them....

He's definitely the kind of guy who buys babies.

"Well?" I ask him. "I don't have a lot of time to fuck around, so do you want this baby and the other two or not?"

"Where is she from? Is she just a peasant baby or–"

"No," I say quickly, but I have to be careful. He might not want to buy the babies if he thinks they're royals. But then, he doesn't want loser babies either. "They're from a good family."

He raises an eyebrow. "And how did you get them?"

I shrug. "Doesn't matter. You want them or not?"

He rubs his chin, thinking about it for a moment before he says, "I'll give you three hundred gold coins. That's it."

I swallow hard. That's a lot of money. I hadn't expected that much. I wonder if I can manage to get more?

I'm not going to press my luck, not with the Alphas closing in on me. "Fine," I say with a sigh. "I'll take it. I'll go get the other two."

"I'll go with you," Stevie insists.

I really don't want him to see Astrid. I don't want him to try and take her, too, but I concede with a nod. I'd rather have the Alphas chasing him than me.

"Fine."

I strap the baby back to my chest because it's easier to carry her that way, and I take him to that house I found in the woods where I stashed the baby.

Instantly, Stevie says, "But there are three more babies here."

"I know. I'm keeping the other girl," I tell him.

He raises an eyebrow at me. "You sure you wanna do that? You don't want to just take the money and be done with it? I'll have these babies on different trains going different directions in a matter of minutes, and whoever you got them from will never, ever see them again."

I look down at her where she's lying on the floor, her fist in her mouth as she looks up at me, wide-eyed. She's not even crying now. It's like she knows I'm her mama now.

"No," I say quickly. "No, this one is mine."

"Whatever," he says. He hands me a bag of coins. I open it and look inside. They are all gold, so I assume they're not counterfeit, but I can't tell how many are in there or their value. I decide to just shove it in my pocket and go.

I split the supplies so that he has some milk and diapers and then help him strap the three little brats to his chest and back. They are already crying. It figures.

"Thanks," I tell him.

"Yeah. But if you get caught, and you tell them about me, just know that I have a wide reach. One of my associates will hunt you down and kill you."

"Don't worry. If I get caught, I'll already be dead," I tell him.

He stares at me for a minute and then turns around and disappears. I hear the babies crying for a bit until he's out of range.

Then, I sink down onto the floor and pick Astrid up. "Guess it's just us," I tell her. She says nothing.

I change her diaper and feed her a bottle. While I'm feeding her, I check the coins again.

"Holy fuck!" I mumble. There aren't three hundred gold coins in here.

There are nine hundred! He meant apiece.

I look down at Astrid's little face. "I should have fucking sold you, too."

She begins to cry.

CHAPTER 11: A MOTHER'S SUPERPOWER

The life of an Alpha King is never dull. There's so much to do, so many people to see, so many things to deal with... the whole thing is just exhausting. Thankfully, there's a perk here and there, like enjoying the company of the lovely woman who is with me right now, feeding me grapes.

Her fingers are so lovely; her nails are painted purple. It's not usually my favorite color, but her delicate little hands sure do look enticing as they grip the fruit gracefully and bring each one individually to my mouth.

Ah, yes. Being the Alpha King certainly suits me well. I must have been completely insane to ever offer to step down for those ridiculous Alphas and the spawn of that breeder woman. Ugh, I shudder at the thought.

No need to concern myself with it anymore, though. My allies are at this very moment attending to disposing of the Alphas and those brats once and for all. I can relax and enjoy the dainty fingers of Miss... whatever her name is.

"One more down the hatch," she says in a sing-song voice, and I smile as I open up for those luscious fingers to deliver me the delicate morsel. It's all so fantastic, and—

"Sire?"

"Ow!"

The screech comes from the lovely woman, whose fingers I've bitten when I just jumped at the sudden intrusion. "What the fuck?" I bellow.

Miss Lovely is running toward the ice bucket holding her finger.

"Who the fuck told you to enter?!" This I say to the rude, lumbering idiot guard who has just run in and interrupted my intimate moment.

He bows low. "My apologies, Your Majesty," he says. "But I have urgent news for you, Sire."

"What kind of fucking news couldn't wait until I've... had my meal?!" I ask.

The guard's eyes remain downcast, as they should be, while he answers, "Your Majesty, there's been an... incident regarding your vehicle."

"My vehicle?" I ask. "Who the fuck is driving my royal car?!"

"I beg your pardon, Your Majesty," he says. "I don't mean your Royal Majesty's personal vehicle. I mean a vehicle belonging to the royal fleet."

"You interrupt me for a car accident?!" I scream at him. "We have people who deal with that sort of thing, do we not?"

"We do, Your Majesty," he says.

I look over to the lovely young lady, and she's crying, still holding her finger. Now I'll have to call for another lovely young lady. I can't stand crying.

"The vehicle in question was driven by Luna Barbara," says the guard.

This gets my attention, and I turn to look at him. At least he's not crying. "Is Barbara dead?" It would suck if she were dead, because I don't know if she's carried out her mission yet. In fact, I don't even know exactly what her mission is. I still don't understand why she didn't tell me.

"Sire, Luna Barbara seems to have been... behaving contrary to the expectations of royalty," he says.

"Oh?" I ask.

"Apparently, Luna Barbara is somehow involved in the kidnapping of the four Alphas' pups," he explains to me.

Kidnapping—is that what she was doing? I suppose one needs to obtain the brats before disposing of them, so that makes sense. She was taking them off to kill them. But it doesn't seem like that went well....

"Is Barbara dead?" I ask.

The guard looks at me like I've lost an eyeball. "Your Majesty, you already—um, no, she's not dead, Your Majesty, although she has been injured in the accident and was taken to Alpha Mark's castle to be detained."

"Detained," I say.

"She's in the dungeon there, Sire," he says.

"I know what that means, you dolt!" I scream at him. "What of the pups?"

"It seems the pups are missing, Your Majesty," he says. "Do not fear, Sire. The four Alphas are at this moment searching diligently for the future heir."

"Shit," I say. The man looks at me strangely again, and I realize I've said it out loud. "I mean, splendid," I say. "All will be fine then." Except that it's not fine, because now I have to find someone trustworthy to clean up after Barbara's mess, and probably someone to take out Barbara too so she keeps her damn mouth shut.

"Yes, Your Majesty," he says.

The man stops speaking and stares at me for a long moment. "Oh, dismissed," I say, waving my hand.

He bows. "Good day, Your Majesty," he says, then he walks off.

I yell after him, "Fetch me another young lady!"

I hear him mutter something under his breath. I must be mistaken because I swear he says, "Fetch her yourself," but that just can't be.

The woman is missing when I look back again. Good riddance.

She was a crier, anyway. I'm sure someone better will come along to feed me my grapes.

I'm surrounded by incompetence! I'll wait until a new woman shows up. Then I need to figure out how the hell I'm going to get rid of the Alphas and those brats now.

There's so much to do as Alpha King.

~

SHELBY

I didn't want Rose to get out of bed, but there really is no stopping her right now. I have no idea how healthy—or not—she feels after having four pups not very long ago, but I can't imagine she's in top shape right now to go running after kidnappers.

At least she has us to help.

The Alphas have—reluctantly—given her their position, so we're all piling into vehicles to head them off at the nearest highway.

Rose is staring straight ahead, a blank expression on her face.

I pat her on the hand. "We will find them, Rose," I say.

For a split second, I see a change in expression, as if she's about to explode into tears, but she pushes it back and restores her determined demeanor. "I know," she says.

I can tell she doesn't want to talk anymore, but I need to. 'Adam,' I say in the mind-link. 'I'm worried.'

'So am I, babe,' my mate says. 'There's nothing else we can do for her right now except help make her feel like she's doing something to help. I'm guessing just lying there doing nothing was more than she could take.'

'Yeah,' I say. 'Any news from anyone?'

'No,' he says, and even in my mind, I can feel the hopelessness in his voice. 'The Alphas are tracking the scent, though. I don't think it'll take long to find them.'

'I just hope they're okay,' I say. 'I... I never even got to meet them.' I would never say that to Rose right now, but that's how I'm feeling. I'm so glad for Adam. He's my rock. 'I wonder what kind of mother I'll be.'

'Is there something I should know, babe?' he asks. There's a hint of humor in his voice, even though it's impossible to be happy at all right now.

'No,' I say. 'Not yet. But someday I'd like to be a mother. Don't you want to be a father?'

'I do,' he says. 'And when the Moon Goddess feels it's the right time, we'll be parents too.'

'I know,' I say. 'I just hope she doesn't wait too long.'

'I love you, babe,' he says.

'I love you, too.'

I look back over at Rose, and she's looking out the window. I can see all her emotions on her face as her eyes cut through the passing forest as though she'll be able to spot her babies even while we're speeding past. Who knows? Maybe she can. Being a mom might be a superpower. You have this life inside you, and you feel it for months; surely there must be a powerful bond there that cannot be broken. Maybe there's more than scent that she can use to find her babies again.

I hope I have that superpower one day soon.

Just then, there's a sudden change in her, and she sits up straighter in her seat, practically jumping out the window.

"Stop here!" she yells toward the driver.

CHAPTER 12: A FAMILIAR SCENT

ROSE

"Stop!" I shout at the driver again, and he practically slams on the brakes, sending Shelby and me flying forward against our seat belts. I don't have time to think about whether or not it hurts as I open the car door and have a look around.

Shelby is out of the vehicle, too. "Rose? What's going on?" she asks me. "Why did you have us stop right here in the middle of nowhere?"

I can't explain to her why I needed the car to stop right here, but I smell something. It's a very faint hint of something that reminds me of the babies. I'm not sure if that's what made me stop, or if it was just mother's intuition, but now that I'm out of the car, I definitely smell it.

"I'm going to walk this way," I say, not really answering her. I take off through the woods, hesitating every few feet, looking around, lifting my nose to the air. Shelby is behind me, keeping her distance but also keeping an eye on me.

The ground is uneven with lots of large fallen limbs, leaves, and scraggly bushes. I step over them, weaving through, trying to pinpoint the scent.

In the distance, I see a little farmhouse. A couple of people are standing outside, either working or talking to one another. I can't really see from here. Like lightning, I take off through the woods, glad that I can run again after all that time carrying those babies. I still have some loose skin that isn't comfortable, but it's a lot easier to move this way.

Not that I wouldn't do anything to have my babies back inside of me where I carried them for all of those months and knew they were safe.

"Excuse me!" I call as I approach. An older man and woman turn to face me. She has a hoe in her hand, and he has a sack. It looks like they've been digging up potatoes. At first glance, it seems they make a meager living out here. I hate to disturb them, but I have to know if they've seen anything.

"Yeah? What's goin' on?" the woman calls.

"'Nother crazy woman lost in the woods," the man mutters.

"Oh, I'm not crazy. I may seem like it at the moment, but I'm not," I assure them. "Did you say you saw another woman in the woods? Recently?"

"That's right," the woman says. "She weren't friendly, though."

"Probably in a hurry with all them bundles she was carrying," the old man adds.

My heart flutters in my chest at his words. "Bundles?"

"Yeah. Squirmy little bundles." he says, shaking his head.

"Babies," the woman corrects him, and my knees go weak. If Adam and Shelby weren't here to hold onto me, I might've fallen on the ground.

"Babies? Four babies? Two girls and two boys?" I ask, shooting questions at them so quickly, they don't have time to answer.

"Didn't check they's diapers, but yes, there was four of 'em," the woman says as tears begin to cascade down my cheeks.

"Do you know which way she went?" Shelby asks as I try to get my emotions in check.

"Toward the village there," the man says, pointing.

"How far is it by foot?" Adam asks.

"Depends on how many babies you're carrying." The man chuckles at his own joke, and I want to attack him for making light of the situation, but he can't know the truth of the matter.

"'Bout twenty minutes, but if you gotta car, that'll shave off half." The woman scolds her husband.

"Thank you kindly," Adam says, reaching into his pocket and pulling out some coins for them.

"Oh, we don't need that for answerin' a few questions," the man says, waving him off.

"Please, take it," I implore them. "If I find my babies because of you, I will gladly give you every penny in the coffers."

"Oh, them was your babies?" the woman asks. "I knew there was something wrong about that woman! We shoulda stopped her, Jethro!"

"What was I gonna do, Velma? Hit her in the head with the hoe?"

As the two of them begin to bicker, we rush back to the car, and the driver takes off for the village. I don't have my babies yet, but I do have an idea of where Retta has taken them.

I decide to let the Alphas know everything I've learned, even though I think they will be mad that I have gone out searching and taken off through the woods by myself.

After I tell them everything, Mark says, 'We're on our way, baby. What's the name of the town?'

I see a sign posted at the border as we enter the city limits. 'Amityville,' I reply, and a cold chill goes up my spine. The name just sounds menacing.

'Oh, shit,' Mark replies, and I bet he doesn't mean for me to hear. He quickly says, 'Uh, that's far away from where we are.'

'It is?" Tristan asks, and I know it isn't because Retta walked there after the car wreck, so they have to be nearby. He just doesn't want me to know that there's something about this town that's bad news.

But it's in his territory, so it can't be too bad, right? Mark is orderly and rules with an iron fist or something. Really, if there are criminals here, they can't be the kind that would hurt babies, right?

I hope not....

I keep my face pressed to the window, waiting for another sign that we need to stop. In the distance, a train whistle blows, and I feel my stomach drop. "Driver, go to the train station," I say. "And hurry."

Without a word, the driver mashes the gas, and we take off, shooting through town on our way toward that haunting sound in the distance. It's as if the train is crying for me because it knows....

The train is leaving–and my babies are on that train....

CHAPTER 13: THE BABY IS GETTING ON A TRAIN!

Mark

'The train!' Rose is shouting in the mind-link to all of us, and she's most definitely in a panic. 'We have to stop the train! The babies are on the train!'

I want to ask her how she knows that, but I don't think that's important right now. According to Adam, Rose had suddenly stopped the car that she was riding in that was flying by an area that turned out to be exactly where Retta had walked by with the babies. Rose is in tune with the babies in a way I can't even comprehend.

So, we're headed toward the train.

Rather than run in wolf form, I thought it would be best that we preserve our strength for whatever assholes we have to fight when we get to town, so I had my warriors meet us at the highway with an SUV, and we're currently driving there—fast.

I wish it were anywhere but Amityville. Yes, it's a part of my pack lands, but that town is a place where the Alphas who came before me had turned away from a bit. We all get busy, and for the past few generations, other cities have needed more attention due to land disputes or other issues. As a result, there were some seedy characters still living there, even though I've been working on cleaning up the place since I took over.

And those seedy characters just might be the type to make money by selling babies.

"What is it?" asks Tristan.

I realize he's been looking at my face, which has probably shown exactly how I feel about Amityville. "I still have a lot of work to do on that town," I tell him. "And there are a few people there I wouldn't trust."

"You think they have the pups?" he asks.

I nod. "Yes," I say. "And Amityville is a hub. If they're on that train, or any others that may have left just moments before, the pups could be anywhere."

The atmosphere in the SUV goes silent again, and I can tell that the driver has stepped just a little harder on the gas pedal. I go to work mind-linking with the people I do trust who make Amityville their home. If all the children are gone… or worse… then it's all my fault for not getting a better handle on the place.

"Stop blaming yourself," says Reece, as if he can read my mind. I look over at him and he continues, "I can see it on your face. We're all Alphas, and we all rule over complex, powerful packs. Not everyone in a pack is the kind of person we'd want to call our brothers. But for most, their families have been with us for generations, so we can't just abandon those people. And many have fated mates. We can't separate those. So we deal with a lot of different personalities and we do our best to keep our people safe overall. You had no way of knowing that it would come to this."

"Thanks," I say, although I don't exactly feel any better. It's pretty much impossible to feel good right now with the pups missing. When little Matthew is safe in my arms, and the rest of the pups are safe with Rose and their own fathers, I'll make plans to deal with the miscreants in Amityville once and for all.

I turn to look out the window as we reach the outskirts of the urban area. From this direction, we'll have to pass through the entire city to get to the train station, where Rose is sure the pups are leaving on a train to who knows where. Unfortunately, our driver has to slow down to navigate the streets, and it feels like a slow crawl as we make our way to the train depot.

'Where are you?' asks Tristan in the mind-link that he's brought all of us into.

'In the city... whatever it's called,' says Rose. 'Where is this damn train station?!'

'Lenny knows the area well,' I tell her. Her driver makes deliveries here often. 'I'm sure he's headed in the most direct way. We're right behind you.'

'I'm not going to wait!' she says. 'As soon as I see a train station, I'm out of this thing.'

'Little flower,' says Tristan. 'Please let us come into the station with you. We don't want to lose you, too.'

'I'm getting out of this car, and I'm going wherever my babies are as soon as this car stops!' she says.

I shake my head at him. There's no sense in arguing with her at this point.

"I had to try," he says.

We all chuckle lightly despite our dark moods. Apparently, now that she's a mother, there's no stopping Rose once she's on a mission, especially one that involves her pups. And I know we all feel the same way right now.

After a few sharp turns, our driver gets us to the train station, and I see Rose there just as she runs into the grand entranceway. As expected, the place is packed to the brim with travelers, and many of them are traveling with pups. It's going to take some doing to find the babies.

Although, four pups together will definitely stick out in a crowd.

None of us wait for the SUV to stop, and our driver does a great job of doing so in such a way that we can all get out quickly and take off in a run. None of us are shifting yet since none of the travelers are in wolf form, but if we don't find those babies within a few seconds, I'm sure this train depot is about to be full of four very angry Alpha wolves.

"Rose!" I yell toward her. She turns around, and I see her face—and my heart breaks. Her eyes are bloodshot and tears are pouring out of her as she looks at all of us in desperation.

We don't even have time to greet each other. Instead, we exchange knowing glances while each Alpha heads in a different direction, and Rose runs down the center, all desperately searching for the children through the packed crowd. I hear Rose's voice call for them over and over again. The rest of us are quiet, carefully scouting out the crowd for signs of the pups.

I catch momentary glimpses of the faces of those around me. Some I recognize, but I don't take the time to offer them more than a quick nod as they give me the sign of respect. I'm sure they can see that I'm in a hurry.

After a few minutes I'm seeing nothing, and I'm still hearing Rose's voice in the background, so finally I ask someone, "We're looking for small pups, newborns. Someone would have four of them."

An older woman's eyes went wide as she answered me. "The royal pups are missing?!"

"Yes," I say. "And we need help finding them. There are two boys and two girls. Have you seen anyone in here carrying multiple children?"

The woman nods. "Yes," she says. "Well, there was a man holding several, but I saw him give them to others. I didn't like the looks of that man, either."

"I knew we should have called the police, Kathy," says another woman standing next to her.

"Next time, I'm listening to you, Mabel," says the first woman.

"Can you describe who the man gave them to?" I ask.

Mabel nods. "Well, there was one man who was even shadier looking than the one passing them out. It must have been a boy because there was a blue blanket."

"The next," says Kathy, the other woman, "was a middle-aged couple. But I don't know which child went to them because that poor dear wasn't even wearing a blanket."

"The third must have been a girl," says Mabel. "She was in a pink blanket. That one went to a very sweet-looking woman who had a wide smile on her face. She must be very kind."

"What about the fourth one?" I ask.

Mabel shakes her head. "There was no fourth one, Alpha."

The rock in the pit of my stomach fell even deeper. Matthew.... If the man only had three pups, what happened to the fourth baby? And we'd seen a blue blanket in the car wreckage, with blood on it....

"Okay," I say. "Do you know where they went?"

"Why, the couple and the shady-looking man, they went on trains going in opposite directions," says Mabel. "Those left a few minutes ago. But the young lady.... Let me see." She looks around the station and her eyes land on someone on the loading platform. "There. There's the young lady, over there!"

I follow her pointing finger toward the platform, where a woman is cradling a pink bundle, cooing softly at the baby—while stepping onto a train.

CHAPTER 14: IS THAT MY BABY?!

Reece

My daughter is here. I can feel it.

From the moment we started tearing through the train station, looking for the babies, I could sense that Reeva was here.

But I don't see her anywhere, and I'm starting to get frantic!

The train that has been loading passengers toots its horn, and I look over to see a young woman getting on the train carrying an infant in her arms. She has a huge smile on her face and tears in her eyes. The baby is wrapped in a pink blanket.

My heart stops beating!

I see Mark and Rose running toward the train, but I am so far away from it, I'll never make it on time.

Instead, I run to the office where they sell tickets and people can ask for assistance if needed. "Stop the train!" I shout at the man who is working there. "Call that train and tell the conductor not to pull away from the station! Now!"

The older gentleman looks up at me as I push through all of the people standing in line, trying not to hurt anyone, but I am in too much of a hurry to pay too much attention to anyone else.

"We can't just stop the train," the man says, scratching his head.

"By order of Alpha Mark, you can and will stop the train!" I command him, knowing Mark would say the same thing if he were over here with me.

"But you ain't Alpha Mark!" he argues.

"No, I am Alpha Reece, and Alpha Mark is right there, running toward that train, so you need to stop it this instant!" I shout at him, pointing my finger in my best Alpha stance.

His mouth drops open, but behind him, I see a middle-aged woman who looks to have some sense about her. She picks up a phone and begins speaking into it. Behind me, I hear the train begin to pull away from the station.

"No!" I shout at the top of my lungs, seeing that the train is leaving but Alpha Mark and Rose haven't made it to the platform yet. The woman is already on the train.

And I'm certain that she has my baby with her.

The train seems to be picking up steam, so I plow back through the crowds again, trying to get to the tracks. If I have to throw myself in front of the moving locomotive to get it to stop, I will. I cannot have my baby daughter taken away to some new location without even trying to get to her.

Just as I reach the tracks, I realize the train is no longer moving at such a great speed. It's actually slowing down. Relief washes over me as I quickly find the closest door and hop up on the steps, banging on the barrier for someone to let me in.

A train conductor pops the door open. "What is the meaning of this?" he asks, but I push him aside, my eyes flying down the aisles, looking for my child.

'We're in the last car, moving that direction,' I hear Mark say in my head.

I notice a woman with a baby, and my heart leaps into my throat, but then I see that the baby is too old, so I keep walking. I see another child, but the ethnicity isn't the same. I keep walking….

I go through one car after another, looking everywhere until I'm in the same car as Mark and Rose, and they don't have my baby either.

"Where is my baby?" Rose shouts, her eyes wide and white. She squeezes onto Mark's arm.

Then, I notice a small woman tucked between the seats on the floor, trying to hide beneath the seat where she is supposed to be sitting, with a large suitcase in front of her, as if she might be able to block our view. I hear a soft whimpering sound. My heart stops beating.

I approach her from the front, signaling for Mark to come from behind. Rose hasn't seen her yet.

Stopping in front of the seat, I say, "Get up. Now."

She doesn't move, so I take the suitcase and jerk it out of the way, tossing it into an empty seat behind me.

"Now!" is the only word I have to say to her.

The girl slides out, her face pale with terror as she cowers before me. I can't think about her at all, though, because in her arms she is holding the most beautiful little creature I've ever seen.

"Reeva!" I shout, bending down and snatching my daughter out of her hands. "Oh, thank the Moon Goddess!"

"Reeva?" Rose shouts, dodging around Mark to come to us. "Is it her? Is it my baby?"

"It's her," I assure her. "It's our baby."

"Oh, Goddess!" Rose takes her from me, and I let her, but I keep my arms around both of them. "Is she okay?"

"She's okay," I assure her.

Reeva knows her mama has her, and she begins to coo, snuggling into Rose's shoulder as tears cascade down my beautiful mate's face. I have tears in my eyes as well. I kiss Reeva on the top of the head and then kiss Rose on the lips. I want to stand here and kiss her forever.

But our work isn't done. We've found one baby. Unfortunately, there are still three babies missing, and I will not rest until we have found them all.

"You're coming with me," Mark says to the woman on the floor of the train.

"Yes, Alpha." She is crying as he tugs her up by her arm.

We head off of the train, and since we know none of the other babies are on this train, Mark tells the conductor that he can go.

Once we are off of the train, I see Tristan and Eli still searching for their children, but I have a feeling they're not here. Mark guides us to the train conductor's office and tells them to stop every train that has left there in the last three hours and to do a thorough search of every one of them for two baby boys and a baby girl, all less than a week old.

Then, we go into a little office with the woman who had my daughter.

She's got a lot of explaining to do.

CHAPTER 15: A LOVE SO DEEP

Rose

The joy of having Reeva back is immeasurable, but it's countered right now by the fear for my other babies who are still missing, and that unbearable mix of emotions is pouring down my face in the form of tears.

I hold my little Reeva as tight as I can. I'm never letting her out of my sight again.

I'm numb as I watch the guards drag off the woman who had stolen her. I don't know what her story is, but Reece is following them into some back room to find out.

As I take a step to follow him, Shelby runs up to me. "Rose!" she calls, and she somehow hugs me and Reeva at the same time. She looks over at the guards and the woman they're dragging away. "Rose, don't," she says. "Let's get you somewhere where you can feed her. She must be starving."

My eyes move back to my baby. She's right. My Reeva's needs come first. I have no doubt that Reece will get to the bottom of whatever that crazy woman was doing with my baby, so I nod. Shelby leads me by the arm to a woman who must work here since she's wearing a form-fitting blue uniform, and the lady has a knowing look in her eye as she directs us to a hallway in the corner. There, we find a room set aside for nursing mothers.

The décor inside the room is nice and calming, exactly what I need right now. I can't nurse my baby when I'm panicking. Shelby guides me into one of the small side rooms, which only has space for the two of us and the baby, and I sit down and get her situated.

My poor baby is starving! It brings more tears to my eyes.

"She's the most beautiful thing I've ever seen," says Shelby quietly, smiling as she touches Reeva's little toes, careful not to bother her as she eats.

It's only then that I realize that Shelby has never even met Reeva— or any of my babies. "This is Reeva," I say.

"Hi, little Reeva," she says. "She is absolutely precious."

"Yes, she is," I say, and that sends a whole new set of tears streaming down my face. I don't know how I have any liquid left in my body at all with all that crying, but thankfully, Reeva is getting some milk.

Shelby grabs me a couple of tissues from the corner of the room, and I wipe my eyes. I look up at her, and it's as if she can read my mind. "You need to leave it to the Alphas now, Rose," she says. "This little girl needs to be with her mother, and you can't run around looking for the others while taking care of her. They have a lead now that they've captured that woman, and they'll be able to find the others quickly, I'm sure."

I nod, but I don't really believe that. I sense in my heart that none of the other babies are in the train station, and I'm scared that the woman doesn't know anything at all. She had looked so happy with my baby. She's probably just someone who bought her so she could be a mother, and she probably has no idea where the awful person who stole them could be. Retta is involved, but I heard Reece mention something to Mark about a man, so they need to find him too.

When I get my hands on that Retta....

"Rose," says Shelby, snapping me back into the present. "Hun, you've got to focus on the baby in front of you."

She's right. Reeva is fussing, and it seems like she's already done eating. I guess that little tummy can only hold so much at a time. I bring her up to my shoulder and gently pat her back as I caress her.

She's so warm, and she smells so wonderful. My heart aches for my other babies, but there's some comfort in holding this little one right now.

Shelby steps out of the room and comes back with a tiny diaper and some wipes. "They're well stocked with supplies here," she says. "I think there are even a few little onesies in the drawer there if you want to change her clothes."

Her clothes.... Only now I look and notice hints of blood splattered on her adorable little outfit. "Oh, my Goddess!" I say.

"Hey, it's okay," says Shelby. "I'm sure it's just splatter from Barbara. Adam said that the Alphas told him how messed up she was."

"But they were in the same car...."

"I'm not helping, I know," Shelby says. "Please, try not to think about it. Let's just think ahead to when you get them all back. Here's a new outfit for her."

I've finished her diaper and am taking off the old outfit and putting on the new onesie, which has a cute little pink teddy bear on it. Shelby grabs the old outfit and throws it away quickly so that I'll stop looking at it.

"What do I do now?" I ask, half to Shelby and half to myself.

"I think you should relax here for a bit," she says. "They have everything you need here, and the Alphas will know where to find you. Adam and some other warriors are guarding outside. You and little Reeva are completely safe in here."

I nod. Safe... I don't care at this point whether I'm safe or not, but I do feel more secure knowing that little Reeva is safe. "You're right," I say. "I need to stay here."

Shelby disappears for a moment and reappears again, wheeling in a small, portable bassinet.

"Wow, they sure do have everything here," I say.

"It's a really modern train station," Shelby says. "Alpha Mark is a great leader and provider for his people, even in this awful village."

I realize that I've never been in a place like this in my life. I've never been a mother before I came to the castle, so I've never needed to go into a private place to nurse, and since I have been a mother, up until now I'd only been with my babies in Mark's castle, never out traveling or in public.

I don't want to part with her, but Reeva is quietly drifting off to sleep. With so much excitement, I know I have to let her rest, and I need to clean myself up a bit as well. The woman in the blue uniform who had brought us here brings me more things, including a pump in case I need it, and directs me to a washroom. I look hesitantly back at Reeva.

"Don't worry," says Shelby. "Auntie Shelby is guarding her with her life. Besides, it's right around that corner. You're not even leaving the nursing room really. Oh, and the Alphas have the healer on the way to check her over. She should be here soon."

My eyes linger for a while on my baby.

"You can leave the door open," says Shelby. "The guards aren't letting anyone else through that door."

"What about the other mothers who need to feed their babies?" I ask.

"They'll be fine," she says. "They're sending them to the other nursing room down the hall."

"Okay," I say, but I still stare at Reeva for a few minutes before I'm comfortable enough to go wash up.

As Shelby suggested, I leave the washroom door open. If Reeva makes the slightest peep, I want to be there for her in an instant. Looking up in the mirror, I barely recognize the woman staring back at me. My hair is a mess. My eyes are red and puffy from so much crying.

A few splashes of cold water help that... a bit. I wash my hands and straighten out my clothes and start to look half-presentable again. I look back up at the mirror and notice something else. That woman in the mirror... she's not the same young woman who arrived at the Black Rock castle so long ago, the one who underwent the exam and learned about her two uterine horns, who shook nervously when the king interviewed her, who innocently bumped into two of the most gorgeous men in the world in the hallway.

This woman... she is a mother. She's strong and determined, and nothing is going to stop her from finding the rest of her innocent babies.

I finish up and walk back out to see Shelby with a huge smile on her face as she watches Reeva sleeping, and the same smile comes to my own lips. I can't help it. Even though I'm still terrified for my other little ones, looking into that sweet little face warms the deepest part of my soul.

"Do you need to pump at all?" whispers Shelby.

"I do," I whisper back. "But I think I need a minute to just relax first."

She nods, and I sit in the chair, which is amazingly soft and comfortable, next to the bassinet, and watch Reeva's little fingers wiggle as she sleeps. The love I feel for her is so intense. There's no way the Moon Goddess will take any of these beautiful babies away now.

I know in my heart that we'll find them. I just hope it happens very soon.

'Tristan,' I say into the mind-link. 'What's happening out there?'

CHAPTER 16: THE WORST KIND
OF ROBBER

Reece

The woman who took my baby is sitting in a small office at the train station, crying hysterically as I tower over her, trying to understand why she would do such a thing.

I've sent the other Alphas away, telling them I can handle this while they look for their children, but Mark wasn't sure. He could tell I was at the end of my rope. I still am, but I am being cautious. As much as I want to rip this woman's head off, that won't help me understand how she could do something like this or help the other Alphas find their children.

One of the managers of the train station, an older man named Harvey, is standing in the corner with his arms folded in front of him. I think he's just here in case I do kill her, so that he can make sure the train station isn't held liable by her family or something.

I decide to take a step back and rethink this situation. Clearly, hovering over her isn't helping the situation any.

"Tell me your name," I say. My voice has an edge to it, but it's not as mean as it could be. I pluck a tissue out of a box from a shelf and hand it to her.

"Be-Be-Bethany," she stutters out.

"Bethany, I am trying to understand how you came to have possession of my daughter. I can't promise you that you're not in trouble, but I can tell you that if you start talking, the chances of you not being thrown in a dungeon to rot for the rest of your life will improve. So... tell me. Where did you get the baby?"

She shakes her head as the tears begin to fall. "I... I... was at the train station, getting ready to get on a train, when this man came from nowhere. He looked like he was really struggling. He had holes in his clothes and he was dirty. He said... his wife had just had a baby, but they couldn't afford to take care of her, and he didn't know what to do. They needed money to pay their bills. They needed money for food. He was crying."

She pauses to wipe away her tears, and I patiently wait for her to continue. "Go on."

She clears her throat. "I said I was so sorry, that I thought that there was a children's home in a town up the track a little ways, maybe he could take the baby there. He shook his head and said he couldn't even afford the train ticket, and he needed to find a way to get some money right away and provide a home for his daughter. I told him that my mistress has been trying to have a baby for a long time and hasn't been able to, so maybe she'd be interested in a private adoption."

I have to bite my tongue to keep from yelling at her that she should never have offered to buy a baby from someone–that not only is it against the law, it's immoral.

"So... he said if I could give him fifteen thousand gold coins, he would be able to pay all of his bills, and I could have the baby for my mistress. I explained to him that that kind of money is over a year's worth of wages for me, and I didn't have that. But he saw the ring I had on. It's the reason I came to Amityville to begin with, to get my mistress's ring cleaned. He said he'd take the ring for the baby. I know that the ring is important to my mistress, but I thought that the baby would be more important. Still, I told him that she wouldn't want the baby without the paperwork to prove it was hers. He said he would get it to me, that the girl was only a few days old, and they hadn't filed the paperwork yet, so he would just list my mistress and her husband as the parents."

"So you agreed to this?" I ask her, and she nods her head as more tears fall down. "You don't think you should've asked your mistress first?"

"The mind-link was out of range, and I don't have a phone," she explains. "I think she would've been happy. But now, she doesn't have a baby or her ring! And I won't have a job, and I'll probably have to go to prison!"

"Yeah, it seems like you really fucked up," I tell her, not pulling any punches. "Did you get the guy's name?"

"Yes! It was Rob Peoples!" she says, confident that she is helping me now.

"Rob Peoples?" I repeat to her. "Did you hear what you just said?"

Her forehead scrunches up and then her eyes widen, and her mouth drops open. "Oh, Goddess! I'm such an idiot!"

"You're definitely not impressing me with your intelligence," I agree with her. "All right. We're going to continue to detain you so if we catch him, you can identify him. What did the ring look like?"

"It has a large ruby in the center with a diamond on either side. The band is gold," she tells me.

I nod, and using the mind-link, I relay the information to Mark, asking him, 'Is there a pawn shop in Amityville?'

'Yeah, there are a ton of them,' Mark tells me. 'I'll send local authorities to speak to all of the pawn shop owners. Maybe good ol' Rob will try to sell it, and we'll be able to catch him.'

That sounds like a great plan to me. I focus on Bethany again. "Did Rob have any other babies with him when he sold you my daughter?"

"No," she says quickly. "I didn't see that he had any other babies with him."

I nod. I wonder if that means that Reeva was the last to be sold or if he had her and someone else was holding the other babies.

Anyway, we need to find this bastard and figure out where the other babies are. While I'm relieved that my daughter is safe, I love

Matthew, Eli, and Trisha like they are my own, and I will do whatever I can to help find them.

Since the other Alphas are out chasing the trains that have stopped, I turn to the man in the corner, Harvey, and ask, "What's the closest pawn shop to the train station?"

"Margie's Hock Shop," he says. "Down on Thief's Boulevard. Two rights and a left."

"Thank you," I tell him. "Keep an eye on Bethany here. Don't let her leave."

"Yes, Alpha," he replies, as if I were Alpha Mark.

I decide to go by and check on Rose and Reeva before I go chase this bastard down. No one hurts my Rose like this and lives to talk about it.

No one.

CHAPTER 17: ESCAPE PLANS

RETTA

I'm starting to think twice about my idea to keep Astrid. Not only did I lose out on three hundred extra gold coins, but I've been having to use up too many of the nine hundred that I did get for the other babies just to buy things for her.

I don't have time to pull over and count what's left of it, so I calculate it all in my head. First, there was the rental car so I could get as far away as I could, then there were the diapers, the formula, a car seat so she's easier to carry, and some cute outfits for her that I'd just seen in a store window the last town back.

I shake my head. At this rate, I'll have nothing to show for it but a cute kid with curly hair. And now, the more she's crying, the more she's not so cute anymore. I should have spent the money on cute outfits for myself. I step on the gas a little harder; I want to put as much distance between Rose and me as possible so she can quit screaming in my head for her babies. I've got enough noise going on with the baby crying. Rose's voice on top of it all is just annoying.

As the engine purrs, Astrid starts to calm down and fall asleep, and I breathe a sigh of relief. Finally, some peace and quiet, at least in the car. I tune out Rose's screaming so I can think. I bet I could have gotten more money for the other babies if I hadn't been in such a hurry before. I can't worry about that, though, because I had to get out of there quickly. It's a lot easier to travel with one baby than four. They'll be looking for someone with four babies.

I pass a sign that says Oasis Creek, which I know is a pretty big town, bigger than Amityville. I should be able to blend in there. Maybe I'll dye my hair and cut it. Or maybe not. I kind of like my hair. Maybe I can just buy a few hats.

If Astrid is worth three hundred gold coins in a rush, I'm sure she's worth a lot more than that in a place where I can take my time to make a good sale. I'm not cut out for this motherhood thing, and it's taking up too much of my money.

I like this car, but I'm going to have to ditch it, since I only paid for two days. I'm guessing that the rental car company will report it stolen when I don't bring it back, and the last thing I need is to get pulled over in a stolen car with a stolen baby. No, I can't risk that.

As I drive into the outskirts of Oasis Creek, Rose's voice disappears from my head. I must finally be out of range! I relax more and look around as I drive through the suburbs. Overall, the city looks like a really nice place. All the houses have pretty yards with pretty landscape designs, and some have nice swimming pools in the backyards with fancy rock waterfalls and barbecue pits. Can I make enough money selling one baby to buy a house with a pool? Eh, probably not. But it's nice to dream.

Soon I'm in the downtown area, and there are a ton of nice-looking luxury hotels. They tower high in the sky and must have hundreds of rooms, so I'll definitely get lost in the crowd staying in one of these. I wonder how many nights I'll get in a nice hotel room with the coins I have left. Maybe I don't have as much time to sell Astrid as I think I do.

In Amityville, I had gone to the seedy part of town to make a sale. I'll probably have to do the same here. But if I ditch the car, it's going to be a long walk to one of these fancy hotels. I shrug my shoulders and keep driving. I'll have to save the nice hotels for when I get all the money from the final sale of Astrid.

The city still looks nice well into the heart of the downtown area, and I'm starting to wonder whether I'll actually find an iffy-looking place where I can find a baby buyer. But just as I'm wondering, there's a huge change in the downtown vibe, and I know I'm in the right neighborhood now. This place gives me the creeps. I'll have to stay in my hotel room after dark.

It doesn't take long until I find a halfway decent but cheap-looking motel, so I park the car a couple of blocks away where I can ditch it. By morning, it'll probably be stolen by someone, especially if I leave the keys in it. If I ever get caught, I'll just say I forgot. I'm not going to get caught.

As soon as I park the car, Astrid wakes up and starts crying again. I open the back door and pick her up out of her car seat to quiet her down. I don't want to draw too much attention to myself.

But when I look into her eyes, and look at that adorable curly hair and feel the way she snuggles up against me, something changes inside me. It's like my heart starts to melt. When she was in the backseat crying or sleeping, it was easy to think about selling her. But now, all I want to do is keep Astrid safe in my arms forever.

No, I guess I won't be selling her after all.

Astrid is mine.

Kelly

I can handle a few more days without much food, but it's really starting to take a toll on the girls. Even though I can't see Heather and Kara most of the time, I can tell that they're getting weak.

I know Eli is looking for me, and he likely has a whole army on the job. I think it's taking so long because he was distracted by the babies' births, but now that the babies are born and Rose is safe, I'm sure he's turned his attention to the search for me.

And in the meantime, it's my job to keep it together and make some escape plans of my own.

I've been working on one of the guards, Randolph. He was really creepy at first, but as I've been working on warming up to him, he's actually not creepy at all. I think he's just been taken advantage of by the other guys, so he tends to try to show off around them. He's different when he's by himself.

Every time he comes in with a little food or water, I give him a big smile, and that's worked well because he's slowly bringing just a little more food and water every time. I think he might be giving us some of his own rations. If that's the case, he probably either feels guilty about keeping us chained up, or he's starting to think I'm really his friend.

Frankly, I'm a little confused about the situation myself. The way we've been talking more, he really seems like a friend. It must be my half-starved mind playing tricks on me. But when we get out of here, I'm going to see about helping him. I don't think he'd be doing all this without someone more powerful calling the shots. That makes me think that either there's an Alpha around or someone very close to an Alpha who's in charge of what's happening here.

I don't understand the value in keeping a few women hostages, unless they know who I am, and they're hoping that holding me can give them power over Eli or the other Alphas.

The door opens, and Randolph comes in again with a big smile, which I return. "Hi, Randolph," I say. "What do you have for us today?"

"I'm not s'posed to talk to ya," he says, but then he lowers his voice to a whisper. "But... I've got a loaf of bread I managed to hide from 'em."

I really don't want to know where he's hidden it, but I'm glad for the food. "Break up most of it and give it to the girls, will you, Randolph?" I ask. "I'd really appreciate it." I give him a big smile at the end, and he quickly does what I ask, giving the girls most of the loaf of bread.

"Don't eat too quickly girls," I say. "Your bellies aren't used to it."

I can see them nodding in the bright light that always floods into the door, the only time I'm really able to see them. They actually look a little better than I expect, maybe because they're munching down on a lot more food than they'd seen in a few days.

I eat slowly, chewing on my smaller portion, which is plenty for me. Randolph has brought a bottle of water for all of us, so I must be getting to him. It's only a matter of time before I ask him to help us escape.

I think he will.

After some pleasantries, he hears someone call him, so he has to leave. I give him one last smile and feel my heart sink as the door shuts, and we're alone in darkness again.

I take my time eating the last of my bread, thinking about the next step in my escape plan.

CHAPTER 18: STOP THAT TRAIN!

MARK

'There's a middle-aged couple on this train with a newborn,' I hear a voice in my mind say. It's the conductor on a train that left the station about twenty minutes before we got there. 'Just doesn't look right to me. They're acting strange.'

'I'll be there in a few minutes!' I answer back. 'Just keep the train stopped, and tell them all it's a mechanical issue, and you'll be going on ahead shortly. Do you have guards on the train?'

'Just a couple, Alpha,' he replies, sounding a bit nervous. 'They don't look too threatening, but I'm not sure what might happen if they try to get off.'

'Can't you lock the doors?' I ask him.

'Well, it's against railroad regulations to lock the doors on a train that's fully stopped,' he explains to me.

I grunt aloud, gaining the attention of the other men that are in the vehicle with me, a couple of guards I picked up at the train station. Tristan and Eli have gone in other directions to investigate other sightings of babies on trains.

'Listen, Bobby,' I say, getting personal, 'I don't give a shit what the regulations say. I'm the Alpha here. Lock the damn doors, and don't let anyone off of that train until I get there.'

'Y-yes, sir, Alpha Mark,' he says, and I can tell by the way his voice is shaking even through the mind-link that I've scared him.

I'm not happy about that, but at the moment, I can't let it concern me. I have to find out if this couple with the baby has one of our children with them.

After about five more minutes of driving at breakneck speed, we come across a railroad crossing, and the driver slows down. "Sir, I can't drive down the tracks, and there's no access road, but the train is about a mile down the road here, between two intersections. I'm afraid we'll have to hoof it the rest of the way."

"Hoof it?" I repeat, trying not to laugh. We are wolves. Why not "paw it"? He just grins at me, though, and I figure this was his attempt at trying to lighten the mood, even though it isn't enough to humor me under the circumstances.

I get out of the car, but I don't bother to shift. If I go to that train in my wolf form, I'm liable to eat someone alive.

I sprint down the side of the tracks, doing my best to watch for hazards, like old railroad ties, broken bottles, and sharp rocks. After a couple of minutes of running, I'm at the train. I pause outside of the door, looking inside.

Something is happening in there. I see the conductor and another man standing on either side of a couple who look old enough to be my parents' age, and they are not happy. The woman is jabbing the conductor in the chest with her finger, and her husband seems to be making demands.

Judging by their clothing, I would say they are pretty well-off, but I don't recognize the man. I wonder if they live in another pack. This train makes several stops in my pack lands and then heads straight into Tristan's territory and beyond.

I bang on the door, and the conductor sees me, recognizes me, and heads over, leaving way for the woman to squeeze out from between the seats, which she does.

It's then that I see she is holding something—someone–in her arms.

"Alpha Mark," he says. "I'm Bobby. Please come in. This couple is getting rather agitated."

"Let me off this train right now!" the woman shouts. "This is my son! Mine!"

I walk over to them, and give her a hard look that immediately makes her stop her demands. Behind me, out on the tracks, there are several guards, ready to shift and eat her face if she doesn't calm the fuck down.

"That's your son?" I ask her, and she blanches, her eyelashes flickering a mile a minute. "No offense, but that must be some kind of a miracle."

Her mouth drops open. "I'm not that old!" she declares.

"Who do you think you are?" her husband barks at me.

"I'm Alpha Mark," I tell him. "And this is my pack territory. Now, who the fuck are you?" I take a step closer to him, and he backs up, hitting the bottom of the seat and folding into it, still stammering.

"We're not from here," the woman says, her face braver than her husband's. "Alpha Tristan is our Alpha and he–"

"Will kill you if you are lying to me," I say, glaring at her. "I'm sure you both understand that Alpha Tristan and I have the same woman as the mother of our children, don't you? And I'm pretty sure that baby you are holding is either my son or Alpha Eli's son, though I can't tell because you have his head covered with that bloody blue blanket." Little flecks of red were visible around the top of the blanket, which made me want to rip him out of the woman's arms to make sure he was okay.

"We... uh...." She looked at her husband who was still sitting there. "We didn't know!" She thrust the baby into my arms, and I saw his face for the first time.

"Matthew!" I exclaimed, melting backward into the seat behind me. It was hard to keep my composure as a powerful Alpha when I'd just been reunited with my missing son. He had been sleeping, but when he heard my voice say his name, his eyes flickered open, and he began to coo.

Immediately, I said through the mind-link, 'Rose, I have him! I have Matthew! And he's okay!'

All I could hear in my head was the sound of her crying. Eventually, she said, 'Thank the Moon Goddess, Mark! Thank you! Thank you!'

'I love you so much, baby,' I replied. 'Now, I have to deal with the people who took him.'

'Okay. Please get him back to me as soon as you can.'

'I will,' I promise her. Then, I turn to the guards outside. "Get these people back to the train station. They've got a lot of explaining to do." Turning to the perps, I say, "As far as I know, it's against the law to buy a baby in any pack lands in the kingdom. You'd better be able to tell me exactly where you bought my son because someone is going to pay for this—and if it's not the guy who sold him to you, well, it'll be you."

CHAPTER 19: MY BABY!

Gene

I swear, I can't get anything done today without one annoying person or another screaming in my head. And this one is the worst because its whiny, high-pitched sound makes me want to hurl.

'What do you want?' I ask, hoping that it'll shut up as soon as she gets whatever babbling she's planning out of her system. I wish Alpha Mark's castle was just a little bit farther away from the spa I'm visiting today. If it were out of range, I'd have some peace and quiet.

'Want? What do I want?!' screams Barbara. It's worse when she's screaming because not only is it high-pitched and whiny, but it's also loud. It's going to give me a royal headache, I just know it.

'That was the question,' I say.

But that only makes her louder. 'This was YOUR mission and YOUR plans for world domination or whatever stupid fucking thing you had planned, but I'M the one rotting in a prison cell, and NOT for the first time!'

'Well, you shouldn't have gotten yourself caught,' I say. It's her fault, the idiot. Why am I surrounded by so many idiots?

'What?!' she screams again, and this time the pitch is even higher, which seems impossible. 'It was your stupid fucking car that flew off the road because the brakes failed—or something—and you're responsible for that. Get me out of this fucking cell immediately!'

Well, the cursing seems uncalled for. 'I'm sure the Alpha will let you go soon,' I say in a very relaxed and comforting way.

'Are you fucking kidding me?!' she bellows, and I'm supposed to be the only one who bellows. 'I kidnapped all four of their brats. Do you honestly think he's going to be nice to me now?'

'Well, just use some of that feminine charm,' I say. That should work. It works on me. 'Who wants a crying, fidgeting little pup when you can have the attention of a beautiful woman?'

She's quiet for a moment, thank the Goddess, so I take a nice sip of my aged whiskey and let it dance on my tongue while I continue with my facial. The flavor is so delightful that—

'You are the stupidest fucking idiot I've ever seen in my life!'

Her hollering makes me choke on my sip of fine whiskey, and I'm starting to get perturbed. I think she even just insulted me. I'm the king! No one insults me!

'Look, you little bitch,' I say. 'You'd better watch what you say or I WILL let Alpha Mark do whatever he'd like with you, including letting you rot in the depths of his dungeon!'

'Oh, really?' she says. 'And what do you think they'll all do to YOU if I spill the beans about whose idea this whole thing was? What if I told them your plot to stay in power even after you promised them that the baby would make one of them Alpha King?'

I set my whiskey glass down. I'm about to get upset, and there's no sense in spilling fine, aged whiskey. 'You said I'd have paws... paws—'

'Plausible deniability,' she says, finishing the sentence for me. I can't remember that damn word.

'Yes, yes that's it,' I say, then I take another sip. She said it herself. The Alphas will never know I had anything to do with taking their brats because Barbara set it up that way.

'You stupid dumbass,' she says. 'That would only work if I played along and said you had nothing to do with it. But now you know everything that went on, and you can't deny any of it, and if you think I'm going to play along after you just called me a bitch and expect me to rot in prison, then you're even stupider than a dumbass!'

Well, I can't argue with that, because I barely know what that means. 'Fine,' I say. 'I'll come get you. Just keep your damn mouth shut until I get there!'

'Make it fast!' she says, then thankfully she shuts up in my mind—for now. I guess I need to gather some guards and make a trip to Alpha Mark's castle. Maybe I can sneak in and get her released while they're all still out chasing around trying to find those brats.

I swear, if you want something done right, you absolutely have to do it yourself.

～

Rose

"Oh, my Goddess!" I can't help but cry out, and the tears are pouring out of my eyes once again as Mark hands our precious little Matthew to me.

My baby is back, and my gorgeous, wonderful Alpha has a huge smile on his face. I am so blessed by the Goddess. I still have two babies out there missing, but I have no doubt that my Alphas will bring them back to me.

Right now, I have to focus on the two that I do have. Poor little Matthew is so hungry that he takes to feeding right away. Reeva starts to fuss a bit with all the excitement in this room, but Shelby picks her up and holds her, so she's fine for now while Matthew gets what he needs.

Mark brushes my cheek with his hand. "I want to stay here with you," he says, "but I need to help the other Alphas find Trisha and Ethan."

I nod, knowing that getting more of my Alphas on the trail of the babies is the priority right now. "I think I'll stay here for now, rather than go back to the castle," I say. "It's more of a central location, and since we think all the babies went in different directions, I think it'll be best. They are so well-equipped here." I look around, grateful for the modern surroundings that make it easy to nurse and care for babies.

The train station employee, whose name I've learned is Lilly, wheels in another bassinet for my little Matthew.

"Thank you so much," I say, "for everything."

"It's our pleasure," Lilly says. She gives Mark the sign of respect and then steps out to give us some privacy. Shelby walks out into the main room with Reeva, so I'm all alone with my gorgeous Alpha.

"Soon, we'll have hours to spend together," he says, still stroking my cheek. "All of us."

I nod. "I know," I say. "I just want us to all be together and home again."

"We'll find them, I promise," he says, then his lips meet mine, gently at first.

I deepen the kiss as much as I can without disturbing Matthew, who seems to be almost finished nursing. Sure enough, he makes a little move and lets out a peep. Mark and I giggle a bit as we part.

"I have to go," Mark says, giving Matthew a kiss on the top of his little head. "You're safe here. We'll bring the others to you soon."

I nod, tears falling again as my heart breaks more for my missing children. Mark takes my hand and squeezes it comfortingly before he gives me one more light kiss, then steps out.

It's so hard to part from any of the men I love, especially when my heart is torn to pieces over my missing babies.

Shelby returns soon with a hungry Reeva, so I hand off Matthew to her and take care of my little girl. I still have a few tears falling, so Shelby hands me another tissue.

"They're going to need another case of these before I'm through here," I say.

Shelby sits down next to me with Matthew and pats me on the arm. "They'll find them soon," she says.

"I know," I say. I'm positive my Alphas will find the babies, but it's so hard to sit here waiting.

"And I am pleased to meet the future Alpha King!" she says. "What a fine little boy he is!"

In my ongoing panic, I've forgotten again that Shelby hasn't met any of the children yet. "He's definitely a kingly one," I say. "Bound for greatness on the throne. We just have to get through all this mess and keep all the bad people out of his life—out of all their lives."

"Everything is going to be fine once they're all back," Shelby says confidently. "I'm sure the Alphas will figure out some better ideas for security so that this never happens again."

"Oh, good Goddess," I say. "Please don't even say that out loud. I don't think I could even live through this again."

"You won't have to," she says. "But being a mother isn't easy, so they'll always be one challenge or another along the way, and I know you can be strong through all of it."

"I'll do my best, for their sake," I say, rubbing a finger on Reeva's tiny cheek. Two of my babies are back, but I need to know whether there's any progress on finding the others.

'Eli, is there any news?' I ask in the mind-link.

CHAPTER 20: OPEN THIS DOOR!

Eli

Life was bad enough when it was just my sister missing. Now, my sister and my son are gone, and I am frantically searching through trains for little bundles of joy wrapped in blue–or pink since Tristan's daughter is still missing–but I'm coming up empty handed.

What's more, everything I've heard through the mind-link for the last hour hasn't been promising. After Mark found his son, the trail has kind of gone cold. We are all searching trains again, but no one has been able to find anything.

Finally, in the early afternoon, I get a message through the mind-link. It's Mark. 'One of the conductors who just returned to the station at the end of his shift said that he did have a small baby boy on his train this morning, but the couple with him had disembarked before I gave the message for all of the trains to stop. He had already stopped at two stations by then, and he's not sure which one they got off at.'

Panic washes through me as I consider what he's telling me. The trains have been continuing on their way after they've been searched and eventually returning to Amityville, so it makes sense that this man is there now, but that means we may have missed my son when he was taken off of the train at one of the earlier stops, so when we searched the train… he was already gone.

'Do we have any surveillance video?' I ask.

'No,' Mark tells me. 'And none of the staff recall seeing where they got off. But I know it was either Woodhaven or Paradise Village. I'll have the local authorities there begin searching for evidence that someone has recently come into town with a child unexpectedly.'

'Good idea,' I tell him. Then, finished with the last train I have to search, I get off and tell my driver, 'Take me to Woodhaven.'

He nods, and I get in the car with the others who have helped me search the train for the babies.

As we drive, I look over a map of the railroad stops provided to me by one of the guards. It seems that the stop in Woodhaven is only twenty miles from Amityville, and by train, that wouldn't take more than fifteen minutes. I've learned that the train in question pulled out of the station on time, so I know about when the baby would've been getting off of the train.

Tristan is in my head. 'I'm headed to Paradise Village,' he says.

'Good because I'm going to Woodhaven,' I reply. Maybe between the two of us we can figure out what has happened to the third baby that got on a train.

But we have a bigger problem. Even if we find this one–when we find this one–we still have one missing, and all of the witnesses at the train station are fairly certain that the man with the babies only had three.

So someone is missing….

I know that Mark is trying to get information from the couple that had his son. I hope that Reece is out trying to figure out where the other baby might be, but that will be hard because we have no leads. Unless Mark can get those people to talk or Rose's mother's intuition kicks in super full-strength, it will be a lot harder to find that last baby.

But I will not give up. I know that, if it happens to be my son that is gone, the other Alphas won't give up on finding him, so there's no way that I will ever give up on finding Tristan's daughter if it's her.

I remember the bloody blue blanket in the car. I remember Mark saying his son was wrapped in a blue blanket. I can't help but wonder if maybe the reason a baby is missing is because one of them didn't make it out of the crash, and since it was a blue blanket... my heart drops. I can't let myself think of that. Wouldn't I know? I feel so connected to my son, my little boy. If he were no longer in this world, I think I would feel it in my soul.

It's sort of like my sister. I know she's in distress, and I hate that I can't get to her myself. I have Trevor and some others looking for her still, but it's not me searching. Yet, I know that Kelly is still alive. I can feel her life force out there in the world. If it went out, I would feel it.

So... I have to believe that my little boy is still alive. I've only known him for a couple of days, but he's already one of the most important people in the world to me, along with his mother. I can't imagine having to say goodbye to him already.

We arrive at a train station, and the moment I get out of a car, I see a man in a uniform that looks like local police marching toward me. Another man in a suit is with him. They look important.

"Alpha Eli?" the one who looks like a police officer asks me.

I nod. "That's me."

He makes the sign of respect. "I'm Police Chief Driver. This is our town mayor, Mr. Velasco."

I shake hands with both of them. "Nice to meet you," I say out of habit. It's not important right now.

"We wanted to let you know that there's a prominent family in our town who just got back from a vacation that took them through Amityville by train. The mayor was invited to their home tomorrow night for a party, and he's hearing rumors that it's to welcome their new son into the family. They are saying, apparently, that the purpose for their trip was to adopt a little boy."

Every hair on my body stands on end. "And there's no evidence that this was what they were doing to begin with?" I clarify.

The mayor shakes his head. "No, not that I'm aware of. They're pretty social people, so I think they would've mentioned it to someone."

I nod in understanding. "Can you take me there?" I ask them.

"Of course. Do you mind if I drive?" the mayor asks me.

"Not at all."

He leads me to his car, and I get in the front, the police chief in the back. I have my guards follow us. All the while, I'm thinking about what I'm going to say to these bastards if they bought my son.

The house we pull up in front of is very nice, but it's nothing like my own home or any of the castles I've stayed in. Still, it's quite clear that these people have money. "What are their names?" I ask the mayor.

"Emmett and Jill Jefferson," the mayor tells me. I nod and we get out of the car.

I walk through a little fence and up a winding path to the large porch, trying not to seem nervous. I need to take charge here. I need to make sure that I can keep myself together, whether my baby is in there or not.

I ring the doorbell and wait. A few moments later, a young woman dressed in a maid's uniform answers. "Yes?"

"May I speak to the man of the house, please?" I say. "I'm Alpha Eli."

Her eyes widen slightly. "May I ask what this is in regards to?"

I clear my throat. "It's in regard to the baby your employers brought home today."

I see panic in her eyes as she must know something is wrong. "I'm sorry," she says. "There must be a mistake. My employers didn't bring home a baby today." She looks past me at the mayor and chief of police. "You should leave." I am sure she's been told to say this.

As she starts to close the door, I hear the sound of a baby crying in the background. But it's not just any baby–it's my baby.

I shove my foot in the door and tell her, "You're going to let me in. Now."

CHAPTER 21: IT'S NOT EASY BEING A MOM

Retta

Wow, it sure is hard work being a mom. Astrid seems to be crying all the time, and I don't know what she wants. I've been giving her formula and following the directions on the can, and then I change her diaper for what seems like a hundred times a day, and she still cries.

I'm doing it again—changing her diaper—when I hear someone pounding on my motel room door. I sigh. I haven't been here long and at least five people have done the same thing. I'm guessing this is someone else who's going to tell me to quiet down. How can I make a baby be quiet on demand?

"For the love of the fuckin' Goddess, woman, shut that kid up!" It's the manager again, with his half-bald head, jeans, and faded rock band T-shirt, and he's standing here looking like steam is coming out of his ears.

"I'm a new mother, sir," I say. It's true; I've only been a mother for as long as I've had little Astrid.

That seems to stir something in him, because he doesn't look as mad anymore. "Look," he says with a sigh. "I'm all for motherhood.

I've gotta mother of my own, 'ya know. But I can't have the screaming around here twenty-four seven. I've got guests who need sleep."

"The only guests I've seen besides me are the ones who stay for an hour with a 'guest' of their own," I say. "I'm trying as hard as I can. Motherhood is tough."

"Ain't there nobody who can help ya, girl?" he asks. "Looks to me like you're a bit out of your league."

"Are you offering?" I ask.

"Hell no," he says. "Just quiet down. Do whatever it takes."

He waves his hand around and walks away before I can say anything else, but I can't think of anything to tell him anyway. I guess he's right, to an extent. I'm out of my league with this mother stuff, and I need some help.

I look at little Astrid, lying there on the king-size bed hollering at the top of her lungs. Even when she's screaming, she's cute. Her little face turns red, and it looks adorable with those dark curls. I love those dark curls.

I go over to the bed and pick her up, and she starts to calm down at least. That's great, but I can't just carry her around constantly. It's exhausting. I know the manager is right, that I need some help, but it's not like I can call up a friend to come show me what to do. I sure can't call Rose.

I had a lot of training as a midwife and how to generally care for newborns, but it's a whole lot different when you're all alone, and you're the only one who can take care of the kid all day and all night. It's exhausting, and I'm running out of energy.

I wish I had my textbooks right now, because I can't say that I paid much attention to the baby care part of my healer training. I just wanted a job for the pack, and they let me train as an assistant healer. I also did some midwife training—that seemed easy since you're only needed when a pup is born, and I figured that wouldn't be very often. So I hadn't really listened when it came to baby care. I just knew the basics about diapers and things.

Well, if I don't have my textbooks, then I'm going to have to go to a library and find some. I'm already dressed, so I grab a few gold coins, hide the rest where I think no one will look, wrap up Astrid, and head out the door, locking it behind me.

By now, the manager is long gone, and the sun is peeking through the city's buildings. There aren't many people on the street, so I walk up to an old lady to ask about a library. When I get closer, I see that she's not really that old; she just looks like she's been through a lot.

"In this part of town?" she asks with a laugh. "Hun, you need to go at least five city blocks north to get to anything like that."

"Five blocks," I repeat with a sigh.

"You can try to get a cab, but there's not many of those around at this hour of the day," she says.

"Thank you," I say, and I start walking. No matter where I am, I'll be walking around keeping Astrid quiet, so I might as well go somewhere to get something done.

It seems to take forever to walk to a better neighborhood, but it's worth it because there's a nice park with some benches and play equipment. "I guess you're a little young for that," I say to Astrid. "But maybe we can stop for a rest at least."

I lay out her blanket on the grass, and she blinks at the bright sun overhead, so I move her over into the shade. She lays there a bit, looking tired, but then after a few minutes, she's crying again. People are looking at me weirdly, so I pick her up and keep walking. I can't afford this kind of attention.

I finally find someone who can show me where the library is, and it's not far from the park. When I get inside, it's quiet—it's a library, after all—so I'm going to have to work fast if I'm going to find a book or two before Astrid starts crying again.

It doesn't take long before I find the right section, and I'm instantly overwhelmed. There's a book about what to expect with babies, and it's huge. Why is there so much to know about babies? Since I'm going to be Astrid's mom forever, I figure I'll need all that information, so I'd better get the book.

I get to the check-out area, and there's a redheaded lady there with glasses staring at her computer. She looks up when I plop the heavy book on the counter. "Sorry," she says. "That's a reference book, so we can't check those out. You're welcome to read it here."

"Oh," I say. "Sorry."

"No problem," she says, then she goes back to staring at her computer screen.

I haul the big book back to where I found it, which is behind a bunch of tall shelves where no one can see me. I'm not really thrilled about carrying the big book all the way back to my motel anyway, so I set Astrid down on the floor, flip through the pages to the newborn care section, and quietly rip out all the pages I need. No one will ever look at this book anyway, and I need the information.

Shoving the book back on the shelf and wrapping the torn pages into Astrid's blanket, I walk out of the library and head back to the motel, which I guess I'll call home for a while.

Nobody will find me there.

And with my new book, I'll know everything I need to know about newborn babies, and I'll be a great mom for my little Astrid forever.

∾

KELLY

"Randolph," I say. "Don't you think those guys are being a bit cruel to you?"

It's been a while, and my idea of warming up to the once-intimidating man is working. He's really a baby in a man's body who just wants to fit in. I think I can convince him to help me and the girls escape, and maybe I'll get him some help, too.

"They is just jokin' around," he says. But I can see in his eyes that those 'jokes' hurt.

"No one should make fun of you," I say. "If they do, they're not a true friend. I think you should come with us and get out of here. I'm sure there are better places for you to be on the outside."

He shakes his head. "Mister says there ain't nothin' out there but mean people who will hurt me and my mama."

"Your mama?" I ask. "Is your mother here with you?"

"Not really," he says. "She's up top."

"Up top?"

"Nah, I've said too much," he says, shaking his head.

I almost had him. Just a little more of this and I think I can convince him to help us, or at least get him to tell me information. "Are they keeping your mother somewhere and not letting you see her?" I ask.

He nods with a sad, defeated look on his face. So they're blackmailing him to guard me. But who? And why?

"Who is 'Mister'?" I ask. "Is that who's in charge?"

"Of course," he says.

"What's his name?" I ask.

"He ain't never said his name to me," says Randolph.

"I see," I say.

"But I've heard the guys talk," he adds, leaning over a bit to whisper into my ear. "They call him Beta."

CHAPTER 22: WHERE'S THE RED HAIR?

Eli

The maid hasn't tried to keep me out since I heard the baby crying. She'd said, "One moment, sir," and then rushed off. I come into the living room, trying to wait patiently by the door while I listen to her speaking to someone in the background.

Most of me wants to tear through the house, knocking over anything and anyone who gets in my way while I'm searching for my son, but a small part of my brain is still saying that I don't know for certain that this couple didn't actually adopt a son recently. This might not be my baby in the house. It could all be a huge coincidence.

I don't think that's the case, but what do I know? Nothing, at this point.

The police chief and the mayor have followed me inside, and they are standing silently behind me while I wait.

Eventually, the sound of a man's voice shouting carries through the living room, and then I think I hear someone crying, someone other than the baby. Maybe it's the maid.

I turn to look at the other two gentlemen, and they are shaking their heads, also unsure as to what we should do, I assume.

When a man appears from down the hall, I take a few rushed steps toward him. I can tell by his suit that this is his house. "Mr. Jefferson?" I ask. "I'm Alpha Eli. I need to see your baby. Right now."

"Alpha Eli! Nice to meet you," he says, extending his hand as he closes the distance between us. He has a smile on his face, but I can tell it's not genuine. He is pretending to be kind because he knows that he is in deep shit. That's my best guess anyway. He says hello politely to the other two men behind me.

"I'm going to get right to the point," I say, trying not to be rude, though if I discover my son is here, rudeness will be the least of his worries. "My son has been kidnapped recently. I hear you have a baby boy. I want to make sure it's not my child."

"Oh," he says. "No, no, no need to worry about that. We bought—uh… adopted our baby in another pack, far from here. In fact, we've had him for a couple of weeks now, so there's absolutely no way he could be your baby."

I can tell that he's lying. Everything about his body language, his tone, his choice of words, tells me that he's lying.

"I'd like to see him, just for peace of mind," I say.

"Well, I'm afraid that's not possible," Mr. Jefferson tells me. "He's just gone down for a nap." He smiles a real douchebag smile, and I just want to punch him.

"I can hear him crying," I mention.

"Oh, well, he just… doesn't want to go to sleep. We're doing the… cry it out method." He is still grinning at me. If I punched him right now, I could get out of this discussion.

"You're doing cry it out with an infant?" the mayor asks, and I can tell by his tone he must have children at home. I don't have any idea whether or not that's appropriate, but I take it from what the mayor has just said that it is not.

Mr. Jefferson clears his throat. "Well, we are new parents. We're just trying to figure it all out."

I am done discussing it. "I will see the baby now," I tell him, and I am using my Alpha voice. He will still be able to say no, if he really wants to, but he should know better than to toy with me.

He takes a deep breath and then looks past me. "Police Chief Driver," he begins. "This is ridiculous. Can you please tell this Alpha, this stranger, to get out of my home."

Police Chief Driver steps up so that he's right next to me. He has a look on his face that makes me think he doesn't want to be jerked around. "Just go get the baby, and this can all be over with, right?"

Sighing, Mr. Jefferson runs a hand through his hair. "I really feel like–"

"Go get the baby, or I will go get him myself," I tell him, my teeth gritted. "And if I have to do it, I can't promise you that no adults who get in my way won't be hurt."

He opens his mouth to protest again, but I step around him, bumping my shoulder against his as I go because he won't get out of the way. "Hey!" he shouts after me. "You can't do that."

"I'd stand down if I were you, Emmett," the police chief tells him, and I am already down the hallway, moving toward the sound of the crying baby.

I know that sound. I know that voice. It's my son. I'm certain of it now.

I arrive at a door that I know is the final barrier between us, but when I turn the knob, it's locked. "Open this door. Now," I say to whomever is on the other side.

"Go away!" a woman shouts, her voice frantic. "You're not taking my baby! He's my baby! I paid for him fair and square!"

I don't give her another warning. Instead, I lift my foot and kick at the locking mechanism. The wood shatters, and the door swings open, revealing a middle-aged woman standing in the middle of a pink nursery, holding a baby against her chest.

A quick glance around the room tells me that this room has been this way for a while, and I have to wonder if maybe they were expecting a baby girl at one point. Whatever happened, I'm sorry for their loss, but I want my son. She's holding him against her, her eyes wide, and as I stalk toward her, she begins to tremble.

"Give. Me. My. Son."

With tears streaming down her cheeks, the woman hands him over as I hear her husband, shouting, coming in the door.

I take the baby and pull the blanket back, looking for red hair.

But this baby is bald.

Completely bald.

CHAPTER 23: I'LL KILL HIM

Tristan

I'm in the middle of Paradise Village, and I'm getting more than impatient. The mayor was nice enough to greet me personally as I got to the town's train station, but now we're stuck here waiting for a train station worker while he looks through his computer for recent arrivals.

I don't have time for this shit. My little Trisha is out there somewhere, and she needs me, not to mention that we still have a little boy missing, Eli's son Ethan.

"We just need to know the time," the mayor asks. I can tell by the tone of her voice that she has run out of patience with this man, too.

"But I need to know the engine number and the conductor in order to know the precise time they pulled into the station," says the man.

"Gerald," says the mayor, "we just need to know if anyone with a baby got off the train here at the station. Now, I'm sure we can ask all your employees—"

"But I can't ask them until I can tell them the exact time!" The man, whose name is apparently Gerald, snaps at her and goes back to his computer.

"I'll ask them myself," I say.

I need to get away from these people before I lose it, so I look around the station for anyone wearing a uniform. There's a woman near the platform helping someone with their luggage, so I jog over to her.

"Have a wonderful day!" she says as she waves off the passengers she was just helping. She turns to me with a welcoming smile that's surprisingly not fake looking. She must really enjoy her job. "Can I help you, sir?" she asks me.

"Goddess, I hope so," I say. "I need to know if anyone with a small baby got off the train in the past couple of hours."

"Baby?" she says. "Well, we get a lot of families passing through here. Let me think."

"This would have been a tiny baby, almost newborn," I say, hoping that helps. My eyes are pleading with this woman to give me the information I need, hoping she tells me that my little Trisha is nearby.

Even though I don't feel her here.

She shakes her head. "I'm sorry, sir," she says. "I know I've seen lots of toddlers come through. There were a few strollers, but none that seemed to hold babies that small. All I've seen are older babies."

"Okay, thank you," I say, and I turn to leave, looking through the crowd again for another worker.

As I walk away, the woman says, "I hope you find who you're looking for, sir."

"Me too," I say in a whisper. I've spotted someone else to try, so I jog through the crowd toward a man in a uniform helping customers near a ticketing booth.

'Tristan,' I hear in my head, and that stops me in my tracks.

'Eli,' I answer him. 'Any news?' I can't explain it, but I feel an even bigger lump growing in the pit of my stomach. I have a feeling this is bad news for my Trisha.

'The baby we're looking at...' he says. 'It's a boy.'

My heart stops beating for a minute and I can't bring myself to answer him.

He seems to understand because he says, 'I don't know if it's him yet, though. They shaved the baby's head."

I can't believe they would do something like that!

'I'll let you know,' he says. 'We'll find your Trisha too. I promise.'

'I know,' I say.

Suddenly, it feels like my legs give out, and luckily there's an empty bench nearby that I collapse into. It takes all of my strength not to burst into tears right now. It's not very Alpha-like, but I can't control these feelings that are washing over me.

I've had so little time with my little Trisha. But every second of it has been amazing. I held her in my arms while she slept so that Rose could feed the other babies, and her beautiful little curls would bounce around just a little bit every time she changed position.

Sitting there watching her, I'd had so many plans for her. I imagined how I'd give her advice about her schooling, how I'd insist that she finish her studies before getting a job. I'd also give her advice about boys—mostly how to stay away from them—even though she'd get mad at me because there was that one that she really liked and was sure he was her mate.

I even pictured myself escorting her down the aisle at her wedding. Those dangling curls would be long by then, framing her face and falling all the way down her back, lying against the dress she'd chosen for her special day. She'd look at me before we stepped forward and ask me if I had any last-minute advice for her.

I think I would say, "If he hurts you, I'll kill him."

The thought makes me chuckle despite myself, and it kicks me out of whatever it is I'm going through right now. I don't have time to feel sorry for myself. Someone could be hurting my little girl right now, and if he or she is, then I just might need to make good on that future advice right now.

I have to find my little girl. She's out there, and she needs me.

~

Retta

I'm back in this cheap motel room, and the first thing I do is set down Astrid on the king-size bed and go look in my special hiding place. If someone has stolen my gold coins, I'm done for.

I sigh in relief as I see they're still there. I'm going to have to be more careful about those. In a place like this, my money isn't safe.

But it's not like I can put it in a bank or something. I can't tell anyone who I am. Even that little trip to the library was a bit of a risk, because people looked at me funny everywhere I went. I just know they were thinking I'm not this baby's mother. Well, I am! Astrid is mine!

I heat up a bottle and get her fed, and luckily, she seems to be as tired as I am after our little excursion, so she settles back in to sleep.

It's time to do my research. I pull out all the papers I tore out of that book, and now they're all a mess, crumpled and torn and all out of order. I guess I should have been more careful.

Luckily, all the page numbers are still visible, so I'm able to sort things into the right order so I can start reading. Feeding, changing diapers—I pass by all the boring stuff because I know how to do that. It's how to keep her quiet that I want to know. Also, I want to be a really good mom that she'll love forever, so I need to know how to treat her right.

But there's nothing about that in here. It's all just the basics, and I already know all that from the stupid healer training. But I need more answers. How do I get her to shut up when she cries? How do I make her sleep longer so that I can get some sleep too? A good mom needs her rest, after all.

Ugh, what a useless book that was and a waste of my time. I'll figure out how to take care of Astrid all on my own.

I can't even imagine taking care of four babies at once. Rose should be happy that I took them off her hands. She can always have another one. Maybe next time, she'll try for one at a time.

Hmm… maybe I'll sneak back once every couple of years or so and get a new one. Astrid would love a baby brother or sister. And if they're not all this small at once, that should be a lot easier to handle for me. Yes, that's a great idea! And I'll still have my perfect figure.

114

I smile as I think about my future—and Astrid's future. I'm going to be such a good mom, she'll never care about Rose or any of those Alphas. Maybe she won't grow up as a royal, but with me, she's going to grow up to be as happy as possible, even without the siblings that I sold. After all, we need the money for a good start in her life. She'll thank me later.

All this reading is making me tired, so I quietly settle in beside Astrid on the bed, careful when I'm climbing on not to disturb her.

I snuggle up close to her and grab a pillow to tuck under my head.

Yes, she's so lucky that she's with me. She's my baby now.

CHAPTER 24: TELL THE TRUTH!

Eli

This is my son. I know that. Even though his head has been shaved, and he doesn't quite look like himself, I'd recognize his face anywhere. Not to mention his smell. I am absolutely one hundred percent certain that this is my child.

Yet, these horrible people are insisting that he's a baby they adopted in another village. I am actually having to consider bringing in a healer to take a blood sample from this baby to do a DNA check to prove he's my child. I want to just take him and go, but with the police chief here, I'm having to do things by the book.

Besides, I do need to be able to prove it on paper.

"I'm telling you, we've had these plans to adopt this little boy for months," Jill Jefferson says, sitting on the couch in her living room next to her husband, Emmett, tears streaming down her cheeks. "The mother contacted us and let us know that she had a child she wasn't going to be able to care for and wanted to know if we wanted him."

"We thought our family was complete until we met little Norman," Emmett Jefferson adds.

My blood runs cold. "Norman?" They'd renamed Ethan Norman?

"That's right. He's named for my father," Jill says.

I am holding my baby, and he has stopped crying, which is further proof that he is mine after all of the crying he had done before I got to him. I don't believe a word they are saying.

"Do you have any proof?" the police chief asks. "A birth certificate, adoption paperwork, a letter from the mother?"

They shake their heads at all of those things. "No, no. She was going to mail all of that to us." These people are such good liars, when Mr. Jefferson makes this statement, even I almost believe him.

"Alpha Mark is on the way," I remind them.

He had been out helping Tristan look for Trisha, but when I used the mind-link to contact him to tell him I needed some help with these prominent citizens of his, Mark said he'd come right over. He should be able to get them to tell the truth since he's their Alpha. He can compel them to do so. Most people who have even an ounce of human decency will cave to such pressure from their own Alpha. I'm not sure if these two have an ounce or not, but we will find out.

"We are happy to explain to the Alpha how we came to adopt our son," Mr. Jefferson says, sounding sure of himself.

"I think we should separate them," I say to the police chief. The mayor nods in agreement.

"What? Why?" Mrs. Jefferson sounds panicked again. "Why would you separate us?'

"I have my reasons." I have already used my ability to suppress their mind-link capabilities, so they won't be able to talk to one another through the mind-link while we are interrogating them. We shall see if their stories are similar.

"The bottom line is this," the mayor interjects. "If the two of you did not actually adopt this baby legally, then that means there are some terrible people out there who stole this child from his mother. Those people need to be stopped. Whoever took the child from his home may have sold the baby to someone else who in turn sold him to you. While we are sitting here discussing this situation with you, not only are we wasting time finding those people, we are delaying this baby's reunion with his mother."

The two of them exchange glances, and for a moment, I think they might cave.

But when Mr. Jefferson is looking at me again, he says, "I'm telling you, we adopted this baby from his mother, and we have done nothing wrong."

I'm beginning to wonder if maybe he believes that. Is it possible that whoever sold my baby to him pretended to be a mother who had had this child and didn't want him anymore? Would Retta have done something like that?

But no, that doesn't make sense. He is saying that he has known about this baby for a while, and Retta only stole our babies sometime in the last twenty-four to forty-eight hours.

With every passing minute, it gets harder and harder to think. We have two babies back for certain. Holding this child in my arms, I'm fairly certain it's actually three.

But Trisha is still missing, and the more time that passes, the harder it will be to find her. Who knows where she is? It seems like she was never brought to the train station.

Maybe Retta sold her to someone different than the person she sold the other three babies to?

Could she have kept Tristan's daughter for herself?

I doubt it. Someone who would steal and sell babies probably has no motherly instincts.

The police chief is still trying to get the couple to speak the truth, but since they won't, I am about to separate them into two different rooms to check for inconsistencies when the front door opens and Alpha Mark walks in.

Immediately, the Jeffersons recoil, dropping their heads in a submissive stature. "Alpha Mark," they both say.

"Emmett. Jill. I don't know why I'm even here. I can't believe you made me stop searching for Alpha Tristan's baby to come here to compel you to tell Alpha Eli the truth about his son. And isn't it true that your company just applied for some contracts with the pack lands?"

Mr. Jefferson's mouth hangs open for a second before he says, "Yes, Alpha."

"Now, why would I be compelled to grant those when you've acted this way? Tell the fucking truth. Now."

Mrs. Jefferson burst into tears, and Mr. Jefferson says simply, "We bought the baby from a man at the train station a few hours ago."

"And?" I ask, needing them to tell me one more thing.

"And..." Mrs. Jefferson says, "we shaved his head. He had red hair. Like yours, Alpha Eli."

Mark shakes his head and says to the police chief. "Lock them up. I'll deal with them later. I need to find my friend's daughter."

With that, I stand, turn my back on these assholes, and walk out of the house, holding my son.

CHAPTER 25: MOVE HER SOMEPLACE SAFE

Gene

I wave goodbye to the wonderful masseuse who'd been working her magic on my back only moments ago and make my driver and my guards head toward that useless Alpha Mark's castle.

Being bothered by fucking idiots is not how I'd planned to spend my day. This is my spa day, the day when all the insignificant peasants clear out of the building so that they can sanitize the entire facility and ready it for my weekly treatments.

They even give it a lovely scent of lavender just before I arrive. It really is an exceptional place.

I've thought about just transforming a wing of the castle into a spa, but an important part of the spa experience is getting away from it all and traveling to this lovely resort setting in the woods. It's positively peaceful, and a king has to take a break from all the work of running a kingdom once in a while, after all.

So there I was just moments ago, just settling into my first massage when that bitch Barbara had screeched into my ear. What do I care if she's stuck in a dungeon somewhere? It's her fault she got caught, so why the hell does it have to disrupt my spa day?

I sigh, remembering how she'd threatened to blackmail me. What an ungrateful bitch. And that's why I need to shut her up myself, once and for all. Everyone around me is positively useless. It's a wonder the kingdom is still standing at all.

"Hurry the fuck up," I tell the driver through the little intercom thing. I'm sure as shit not going to breathe the same air as the useless bastard, so there's a thick, bulletproof partition between us. He's just another moron in a long line of morons making sorry attempts to serve me, their incredibly wonderful Alpha King.

"Yes, Your Majesty," he says.

I just grunt and let go of the button. I have more important things to do than talk to him, like figuring out my plan for offing that little bitch, Barbara. She sure is a looker, though. It's a shame she has to meet her demise so young. We could have been so good together.

Ah, well. It just wasn't meant to be.

My plan is fairly simple, which is the genius behind most of my plans. I just keep everything really easy, mostly so I won't forget what the hell I was supposed to do. Why make things complicated?

All the useless Alphas are off in different directions looking for their little brat pups, so no one is in charge back at Mark's castle that I need to worry about. I'm the Alpha King, and I can do what I want wherever I want, so those idiots will just have to let me in the door, then I can march down to the dungeon and slit her throat. I'll say it was self-defense.

Yep, that sounds like the perfect plan to me.

Thankfully, the spa is a lot closer to Mark's castle than my own castle, so it doesn't take long to get there, now that my driver is actually doing his job driving the vehicle instead of spacing out, or whatever the hell he was up to before.

We pull into the courtyard driveway, and as always when I'm out in my kingdom, my adoring subjects are thrilled and impressed with my presence. I can tell by the looks on their faces that they're upset that I hadn't announced my visit earlier so that they could have proper preparations in place for my arrival. Maybe they wanted to decorate and have a parade.

There's no other explanation for the looks of shock on their faces.

I sit here once we roll to a stop and wait for my people to get their acts together. They have one job, and they can't even do that right. They're supposed to get my step, which helps me get out of this SUV in a more graceful manner, and ensure that it's sturdily attached to the ground, however the hell they do that.

As the king, I cannot be seen tripping or stumbling out of my vehicle! I can't help it the damn thing is so high off the ground.

Finally, after what seems like hours, they've got their shit together, and someone opens the door for me.

"Your Majesty," says one of the men from Mark's castle. "Welcome to River Pack. We're thrilled to see Your Majesty, but we were not informed of your impending arrival."

"Of course, you weren't, you dolt," I say. "I'm the Alpha King! I don't have to get my schedule approved through you or anyone else."

He sucks in his lower lip for a second and then continues, "Of course, Your Majesty. Our Alpha Mark is not here to greet you. He, unfortunately, had a family emergency to attend to. Otherwise, he would be happy to entertain you personally, I'm sure."

The man is standing in my way, blocking my perfect exit off the step. In fact, looking around, I'm noticing quite a few of Alpha Mark's people standing between me and the entrance to the castle. "No matter," I say. "I'm not here to see that idi—to see Alpha Mark anyway. My business is in your dungeon. I'll thank you to take me there immediately."

The man takes a deep breath and sucks in his bottom lip again. Why does he keep doing that? "I'm sorry, Your Majesty," he says. "But I'm afraid that I can't let anyone into the dungeon without express permission from Alpha Mark."

"What?!" I bellow in my most impressive Alpha voice. "I am the Alpha King! There is no place in my kingdom where I am not free to go whenever I please!"

"Yes, of course," says the man.

Finally, the idiot will be submissive. I hate having to use my Alpha voice. It makes my throat tickle, and I hate tickling. Unless it comes from that beautiful masseuse with long auburn hair....

"But, Your Majesty," he says, "I'm afraid we'll need for the workers to finish first."

"What workers?" I ask.

"Well, we have some renovations going on down there, and right now, the entrance is blocked until the workers finish up. It would be very dangerous to go down there now. You may trip and fall! Perhaps you would enjoy some refreshments in our lounge while the workers get things in order for you. We have quite an exquisite VIP lounge with all the drinks and food you could possibly desire."

"I'll be the judge of what I desire!" I say.

But a nice, stiff drink does sound good. And so does some food. That Alpha Mark seems like a well-nourished fellow—he must have a great cook here.

"I'll permit you to escort me to the lounge. But do tell those workers to make it snappy! I have important business to attend to."

"Of course, Your Majesty," says the man.

He moves out of my way a bit more so I can step down in a more dignified manner, and for some reason, the crowd of people parts to create a path toward an area that, as I remember it, is opposite the direction of the dungeon. I guess they just need more time. Good thing I'm hungry and thirsty.

The man—whatever his name is, that's not important—guides me to the VIP lounge, which isn't as great as my own quarters, but I have to admit it's impressive. A couple of lovely young ladies show up with big smiles on their faces and plates of delicious-smelling goodies that make me almost forget why I'm here in this miserable castle.

I'm especially enjoying the little mini sausages with the little sticks in them. They're simply a delight, especially when one of the ladies feeds them to me.

I've spent a few moments in a delightful conversation with a beautiful blonde when I start to hear that screeching sound in my head again. Thankfully, since I'm present in the castle where it's coming from, I'm able to suppress it with my Alpha powers by shutting down Barbara's mind-link.

I'll go kill the little bitch when I'm good and ready.

~

MARK

'What?' I ask with a sigh.

Carlton, my Beta, is messaging me in the mind-link. I'm just leaving the Jeffersons' house, where I had to take time out of my search for Tristan's daughter, Trisha, to make those baby traffickers admit they had Ethan, Alpha Eli's son, and now I'm getting news that the idiot King Gene is at my castle trying to get into the dungeon.

'I'm sorry, Alpha,' says Carlton. 'Luckily, it's really easy to distract him. We're trying to get him drunk so he just forgets where he is altogether. I'm going to owe Veronica and Beverly big time, though.'

I chuckle a bit. 'Thank you, Carlton,' I say.

I don't doubt that Gene wants to get to Barbara, and while I'd be glad to have the world rid of her presence for what she did to my family, I know that if Gene wants to get to her, then she must have some good information on him that could help us get rid of Gene once and for all. Since that's the case, I need to protect her for the time being.

Eli is busy getting Ethan back to Rose as quickly as possible, and Tristan is most likely losing his mind with worry for his own daughter, so I don't want to bother either of them.

'Reece,' I say in the mind-link. 'Do you have any people left at my castle? People you can trust?'

'Yes, of course,' he says. 'A whole contingent of them. Why? What's up?'

'I need you to help me move Barbara to someplace safe.'

CHAPTER 26: LET HIM KILL HER

Rose

I have three babies.

Three babies in my arms. Two sons and a daughter.

I love them more than anything in the universe. I love them so much my heart is heavy with emotion. Ethan does look different without his bright red hair, but I know that will grow back... eventually.

But... there's also a hole in my heart, and that feeling of sharp pain in my chest will never go away when one of my children is still missing.

Granted, I have three babies, and that makes me happy, but my sweet, curly-headed, bright-eyed Trisha is not here. And without my little girl in my arms, I will never, ever be complete.

Tristan is still out there searching for her, but he hasn't had any luck. Mark and Eli are going to help him now that they've found their sons. It took a bit of time for Eli to get those beasts who bought Ethan to admit it, but now, he has some of his people interrogating them, along with the chief of police from the town where Ethan was recovered.

So far, from the people who bought the boys and Reeva, all we've been able to gather is that a man sold them the babies. We have a decent description of him, and Mark has sent that information out with as many guards as he can get to come here to march through Amityville as he is convinced that this is where the man is located.

But if he is any kind of good criminal at all, he's probably already left town one way or another.

And I'm guessing Retta has left town, too. Is it possible that she still has Trisha with her? I don't know. I sort of hope so because then, when we find my daughter, we will find the person who is responsible for all of this, but I also can't imagine my daughter with that evil woman.

At least she knows how to take care of babies. She has trained as a midwife and a nurse, at least, that's what she convinced me of. I still curse myself for being so freaking stupid! How did I let someone who has always hated me fool me into letting her near my babies?

Ethan was so hungry, he's been nursing nonstop for almost thirty minutes. Matthew decided he wanted to eat, too, so I'm feeding the boys while Reeva sits on my knees, sleeping. I know Shelby is itching to pick her up, but I haven't let her yet. I want to hold all of my babies–but I still can't do that.

Mark thinks we should go back to his castle now, especially since it seems like Trisha was never at the train station. But I'm afraid to go back there. I don't want to return to the place where my babies were taken from me.

A tear comes to my eye and Shelby sees it as it spills over. "I'm sorry, Rose," she whispers, squeezing my hand. "We'll find her. Look how good of a job the Alphas have already done at finding these three."

"I know," I say, and I really do believe that it's true that we will find her. But I just keep thinking about how I could've been a better mother and prevented all of this from happening.

"I should've been more careful," I say, beginning to sob again. I don't want to disturb the babies, so I try to hold back, but it's hard. I feel so overwhelmed with sadness, thinking about how badly I messed up.

"Rose, this isn't all your fault. A lot of people messed up missing this. You can't blame yourself." Shelby takes Ethan from me as he's finished and just lying there. She lifts him over her shoulder to burp him. She's going to be such a good mother one day.

"I'm not sure I can go back to Mark's castle," I whisper as I fix my top. "I'm not sure I can do it. I have the wonderful memories of birthing my babies there, but then, I almost died, and then my babies were stolen from me, and all of these guards were slaughtered. It was just so horrible, and going back there may make me relive all of the horror."

"I know," Shelby says, patting my son's back. "You don't have to go back there if you don't want to. All of the other Alphas have castles. Granted, some of them are further away than others. But eventually, King Gene is going to have to either step down or be defeated because your son is the next Alpha King, and in the meantime, Mark will be in charge of the kingdom. So chances are that you will be able to return to the castle soon enough."

I think about that for a moment. Do I even want to return to King Gene's castle? He wanted me killed while I was there, and I'm guessing that he still does. In fact, I have to wonder if Retta and Barbara weren't motivated or even paid by Gene to do this.

Suddenly, I do want to go back to Mark's castle. I want to speak to Barbara myself.

"Shelby," I say. "I think... maybe I should speak to Barbara."

Her eyes bulge. "Why would you want to do that?"

"Because... I want to know if King Gene put her up to this," I explain. "Where's Adam?"

"He's helping with the search," she tells me. "But Rose, I don't think you need to talk to Barbara about that."

I hear a tone of caution in her voice. "Why is that?" I ask her.

"Because... a few minutes ago, Adam let me know that we had another visitor at Mark's castle."

My stomach rolled over, and I took a deep breath before I asked the question I was pretty sure I already knew the answer to. "Who is it?"

"King Gene," Shelby told me, her eyes locked on mine.

"Was he there to try to break Barbara free?" I would be so angry if she got away with this.

Shelby shook her head. "No. Mark doesn't think so. He thinks he's there to kill her."

I wasn't sure how I felt about that, but part of me wanted to say, "Let him."

CHAPTER 27: IT'S ALL GONE

KELLY

I can't really tell how much time I've been here in this mostly dark cave, but I can tell that it's been quite a while now. That can only mean one of two things. Either Eli has been captured himself and can't come to rescue us, or something terrible has happened to Rose or the babies that has caused a delay.

It is very possible that he was captured. After all, if they got to our car, whoever is behind this may have ambushed Eli's car first. If that's the case, they're keeping him in a completely different facility, because I can't sense him here, and I can't reach him by mind-link.

But I really don't see that happening, so I'm terrified that there's something wrong with my niece or nephew—at this point, I don't even know which—that's preventing Eli from finding us. I can't imagine what that could be, but I do know that there are plenty of people out there who might want to harm the heirs to the throne.

I slide myself down to the ground as I think about the babies. I wish I could have been there when they were born. Eli had been so excited, and nervous, about being a new father. I wonder if the little pup has his or her father's red hair. If they do, I know that Eli is just loving it. He's so proud of our family heritage.

I hope and pray to the Moon Goddess that I'll get out of here and will finally get to meet the babies. I'm working hard to stay positive, but the more time passes, the harder it is to keep my chin up. The only thing that's helping is knowing that I need to stay strong for Heather and Kara. Well, that and the glimmer of hope that I'll meet my brother's little pup one day.

My first step, though, is getting Randolph on my side, and that's what I'm going to do as soon as he walks through that door.

It's not a long wait before Randolph finally arrives with our food and water. I'm always grateful because I don't know exactly how strong these girls are, so I'm just not sure how long they will last. Luckily, he's brought a lot of bread this time, and while it's not ideal, at least it's getting some calories into us.

"Thank you, Randolph," I say with a smile, and I let my eyes linger on him just a few seconds more.

"It's my pleasure, miss," he says.

"Now, you know you can call me Kelly," I say.

"Right," he says. "I forgot. Kelly, it's my pleasure."

I smile back at him for a bit and get some more food in me before I say, "It sure would be nice to get out of here once and for all."

I let that float in the air for a bit because I could tell by the look in his eyes that he was mulling it over.

Then I lower my voice for the next suggestion. "There are three of us, plus you, and you're the biggest of all the guards. If we all teamed up, we could overpower them all and get out of here."

His eyes went wide. "But they're just little girls," he says in a whisper.

I have him now. He's considering it.

"Yes, but they're strong girls," I say. I don't know Kara well, but I've spent enough time with Heather to know that she can hold her own in just about any situation. "And we've been getting stronger with you bringing us food."

I go back to eating my big piece of bread and drinking my water while Randolph glances back to the door, then looks back at me.

We are both quiet for several minutes as the idea settles into his mind.

Then he looks at me and nods. "Okay, I'll help you get out of here."

~

RETTA

Ugh! I'm so sick of this baby crying all the time. I know babies cry, but this is getting to be ridiculous. The motel manager has been here three times already today, and I know that if he has to come back, I'll be right back out on the street.

I carry Astrid back and forth across the ugly, dirty carpet, willing her to be quiet.

When she finally settles down, I lay her on the king-size bed and put some pillows around her. Stepping back and looking at her, I admire how adorable she is with these little curls.

But cute curls don't pay the bills.

My stash of gold coins is quickly disappearing between paying rent on the motel, buying food for me, and buying formula, diapers, and new clothes for Astrid. At this rate, I'll be drained of funds before the end of the week, so there's only one thing to do.

It's time to go sell her.

Lucky for me, I'm already in the sleaziest part of town, where there will most definitely be someone willing to buy a baby—with no questions asked. A cute little girl like her could get a fortune on the open market, probably way more than the 300 coins per baby that jerk gave me for the other three pups.

The first step is finding a better spot for my gold coins, because I don't want them gone when I get back. I know I can get a lot for Astrid, but I don't want to get it at the expense of losing all the rest of my money.

Moving the carpet, I feel along the floorboards—which is a disgusting task in this filthy place—until I find a loose one that I can pry up easily enough that when I put it back down, it'll look undisturbed. There's a perfect little spot for the bag of coins, almost as if it were made for them, so I tuck them in, replace the board, put the carpet back down, then pack up Astrid for our little trip.

I try not to look her in the eye. As a mother—at least as a temporary one—I've become too attached to the little girl, so I don't want to do anything that'll make it harder for me to get rid of her. Once ready, I head out the door and carefully lock up my motel room. No one will get to my money, that's for sure!

I walk in the opposite direction from the way I went to get to the library, since I know the city gets nicer that way, and head deep into the worst part of town.

There are some working girls on the corner; I can tell by their clothes. They don't look happy to see me at first, but they warm up a bit when they notice Astrid. I guess at first, they are worried I'm some new competition until they see her.

"Anyone know where I might find someone... interested in getting a baby?" I ask. It's a bold question, but I don't have time to play games, and it's not like these women are sticking to the law themselves.

They look at me funny, but the one with an obvious blonde wig points to a bar across the street. "You can probably find Max in there. He handles... lots of things," she says.

"Thanks," I say, heading across the street. The bar is quiet inside except for a couple of guys downing beers at the bar. "Is Max here?" I ask the bartender.

He looks at me hard, as if he's studying me, then he visibly relaxes and nods toward a dark corner. I now notice that someone is sitting there in the shadows. I nod back to the bartender and head over to see Max.

"Hi," I say, and he looks at me just about the same way everyone else is doing. The man has a long, scraggly beard and looks like he hasn't showered in a while. He doesn't say anything, so I continue, "I... I need to get... to find someone who can take this little girl."

"Girl, huh?" he says, then a terrifying smile creeps up on his face, and his eyes start to sparkle.

I instantly feel the hair on the back of my neck stand up.

"I think I can help you with that," he says. He scratches his nose, looks down at the table, then looks back up to me. "I can get you 400 for her."

I try to keep my face calm since this is more than I got for the other babies, but I have a feeling she's really worth a lot more. "Do you think you can 'get' 600?" It's risky, being twice as much as before, but I'm sure couples are willing to pay more than that.

"You drive a hard bargain," he says. "But sold. I'll get a girl over here to take her. And I'll go get your money."

"Thanks," I say.

I stand here for a while, bouncing Astrid around to keep her quiet, until one of the working girls from across the street walks in.

"I'll take her," she says.

I'm about to hand her over when Astrid looks at me with those pretty little eyes. "Do... do the couples usually come in here to pick up the babies?" I ask the woman.

She laughs. "Couples?" she says. "Ain't no couples involved. Max buys 'em for his own stock."

My eyes open wide and, instead of handing Astrid over to the woman, I pull her back closer to me. "What?"

"You heard me," she says. "He keeps 'em for himself."

I shake my head almost involuntarily and back all the way out the bar's door. At that point, I turn around and break into a run. I get several blocks away before I slow down, and thankfully no one is following me.

Back at the hotel, I lay Astrid down on the bed and heat up a bottle for her. What a horrible man! I guess I'm going to have to be picky about who I sell her to.

After feeding her and getting her to drift off from our adventure, I loosen the floorboard to get to my coins. I need to count them one more time to see how many days I have left since it seems it'll take longer to sell Astrid.

My sack of coins is gone.

CHAPTER 28: I'VE GOT THIS

Rose

"Rose, I just don't think it's a good idea," Reece is saying as I get help from a few of the train station employees in packing up the belongings that have been delivered to the babies and me since we arrived here. That includes four car seat carriers. Only three of them currently have babies being wedged into them, and that makes my heart heavy.

"I want to speak to her," I tell him, shoving some spare diapers into a bag.

The people of Amityville might have a reputation for being miscreants, but they really came through when they heard that the royal babies were at the train station. Since then, many of them have sent out search groups as well. They're trying to find leads to give to Alpha Mark to let him know who might be the one who bought the babies from Retta.

I have a feeling, though, that Retta still has Trisha. If only she would answer the mind-link…. She has been ignoring me since the moment she first realized I knew what she was up to.

"If you go back there now, you'll have to face King Gene, and I cannot let you do that alone, Rose. He's still too dangerous."

"The man doesn't know how to tie his own shoes! Haven't you noticed? All of his shoes are either Velcro or boots. He only wears slide-ons."

Reece starts to laugh a little, but then he sees my face and realizes I don't think this is funny. "You're right, Rose," he says. "I know that Gene is an idiot, but we have to imagine he still has powerful men working for him that could cause some damage if they wanted to. So I really think it would be best if you didn't get anywhere near him."

"Let's send him away, then. Let's trick him into thinking that Mark has already moved Barbara. I mean, wasn't Mark talking about doing that anyway? I know you need to get back out there and help Tristan look for Trisha, but I think we should handle this first. Or Adam can do it."

Reece opens his mouth, takes a deep breath, and lets it out. "Fine. I'll work on fooling King Gene so you can talk to Barbara, but we need to figure out a way to get you back to the castle safely. So far, Kelly alone has been involved in two wrecks that caused her to be kidnapped. The car the babies were in wrecked. Clearly, people don't know how to drive around here, or there are just a lot of people who want to cause people to wreck so that they can kidnap them."

He does have a point. "I am sure that the armies you guys have standing by can spare some people to escort us back to Mark's castle, and these babies will not be leaving my sight ever again, until they are twenty-one years old."

"What about when they go to school?" he asks me with a smirk on his face.

I do not laugh. "No."

"Okay," he says. "We'll sort it out. I just... someone here in town has to know where the man who bought the babies from Retta is, wouldn't you think?"

"I would think. Is it possible Gene is threatening people to not tell us?" I ask. It doesn't make sense. Amityville is not that big.

"I don't think he's that smart," Reece states. "But it would be nice to know why this guy didn't buy all four babies. Was there some reason he didn't want Trisha or did Retta want to keep her?"

I fold my arms under my chest and glare at him. "Are you saying there's something wrong with my little girl?"

"Absolutely not!" he says, holding his hands up in defense. "No, I just think that maybe he could only take three. Or maybe he didn't have enough money to pay her everything she wanted, so she went somewhere else. Who knows?"

I continue to give him a mean glare for even implying that maybe there's something wrong with my little girl. Every evil baby-buying creep would want my daughter.

"All I know is, I've made up my mind. Even though I didn't think I'd ever want to go back to Mark's castle, the scene of the crime, I want to talk to Barbara, and I want to talk to her now. Then, we can go somewhere else. Like... your castle or Tristan's or something." I know Eli's far away, so I don't mention it.

"Fine, darlin', whatever you want." He has his hands on my upper arms, and I think he's going to kiss me. I'm not sure if I want him to after what he said about Trisha not being worthy of being bought, but when his lips come down softly on mine, I'm glad that he's here. I lift up on my tiptoes to better reach him.

Shelby clears her throat. "The babies are ready to be loaded into a car. If we have one."

"Yes, there's one out front," Reece says. "I'm in the process of sending King Gene off to my castle after a fake Barbara. We'll just have to see if we can get him to leave before you arrive. But Rose, you need to be careful when you face her. I mean, she might be locked up in prison, but she's still a deceptive woman who is likely to lash out and hurt you."

I glare at him even more deeply now. "I will rip her fucking head off and shove it up her ass."

He nods. "I think... you've got this handled then."

I turn and pick up Reeva and Ethan in their carriers, and Shelby takes Matthew, and we head out the door, with staff from the train station carrying my other bags. Dozens of guards are waiting outside to escort us to the waiting SUV. Reece follows along behind us to make sure we get in the car okay. I know he thinks he should take us back to the castle, but Adam is with us now, and I know it'll be all right. As long as Shelby is with the babies while I'm confronting Barbara, everything will be just fine.

And if Gene is still there when I arrive, I'll rip his fucking head off, too. I'm not afraid of him anymore. I know what it's like to lose everything now, and it hurts like hell. But I also know that what's lost can be found. And I will rise from the ashes.

Like a fucking Phoenix.

CHAPTER 29: BABY FOR SALE, CHEAP

RETTA

My heart is racing, and there's a rock in the pit of my stomach big enough to make me want to throw up. Desperately, I pull up another floorboard, thinking maybe my money fell to the side or something and it's still there.

But there's no sign of my money bag.

I feel like I can't even take a breath. I've never felt this out of control in my life. I look around the room, trying to remember if maybe I didn't really put the gold coins into the floor like I'd meant to. Maybe my mind is playing tricks on me.

I pull out all the drawers in the dresser, look under the bed, search in the closets... I look everywhere, and that beautiful sack of gold coins is nowhere to be found.

To make matters worse, all my rustling around the motel room has made Astrid wake up, and she's starting to cry. I pick her up to try to get her to quiet down before the manager or the neighbors start complaining.

Oh, no, the manager... I remember that I'm supposed to pay him today for my room, so he will probably be by soon, and he'll show up even sooner if Astrid doesn't quiet down. I don't have a single gold coin left to pay him....

Bouncing Astrid against my shoulder, I use my one free hand to make her a bottle. There's barely any formula left, just enough for this one feeding. Looking over at what's left of the package of diapers, I start to panic even more. There are barely enough left to last for a single day.

I lay Astrid down on the bed to feed her, because that's easier. At least she'll quiet down with a full belly, even though that might be the last bottle she'll get for a while. She finishes up, and I pick her up to burp her, then I set her back down, and she closes her eyes again, thankfully.

I prop a couple of pillows around her and sit down on the chair, the only one in this tiny motel room. I need to come up with a plan. There's no formula left, and it's not like I can feed her myself since I'm not her real mom, so that's a huge problem. Then there's the matter of the diapers, and of course, the room rent I'm supposed to pay today.

It's looking like I have no choice left.

I take one last look at Astrid sleeping soundly, her little dark curls bouncing with every move of her head. She's adorable, and I want her to be mine forever, but I need to prioritize things right now.

If I don't get rid of her and get some money for her now, I'm going to starve. I'm not going to let that happen. She's cute and all, but my life has to come first.

So, I make up my mind and decide it's best to get the hell out of here before the manager shows up. I'll just take everything I own and never come back. It's not like I have a lot with me, so it doesn't take long to gather everything. The last thing I do is pick up Astrid and walk out the door.

Luckily, no one is around, so I get out of the room before the manager can see me.

And I head down the street... back to Max in the bar.

There are a few more people here when I arrive, and they all eye me a little funny for carrying a baby into a bar, but that doesn't last long as they turn the other way. I guess everyone around here knows what Max is up to.

There's a man in the corner I've never seen before, and frankly, he doesn't look like he belongs here. Everyone else in here—in this whole neighborhood, really—looks like they've been through a long life, even those women on the street corner who must be around my age. I guess a hard life really does age people quickly.

This man… he's got some really beautiful blond hair and blue eyes, and he's just sitting quietly in the corner watching people, sipping on a glass of something. Maybe he's new to all this.

Then my eyes meet Max, and a sense of dread washes over me. I don't want to sell Astrid to such an awful man, but I have no choice. I can't keep taking care of her without money, and I can't get money unless I sell her. I'm sure her life won't be too awful. After all, those women on the street seem nice enough. Maybe they got sold to Max as babies too.

I can't think about Astrid anymore, and that's really hard to do while she's still in my arms, so I hope Max just buys her and they take her away as quickly as possible.

"Well, would you look at who's back?" Max says with a bit of a drawl, his mouth forming a smile that adds to the dread I'm already feeling. "Change your mind, little lady?"

I nod, having a hard time getting the words out of my mouth. But then I remember how desperate my situation is right now, how I'll starve if I don't sell Astrid, and I say, "Yes. I'm afraid I do need to sell her. Four hundred, right?"

Max laughs—not as if he'd heard something funny, but in a strange sort of half-sneering way that reminds me of that pit in my stomach. "Little girl," he says. "That offer is no longer valid."

"No longer valid?" I repeat his words. I know what he means, but right now I'm just not able to accept what he's just said. "You don't want to buy her?"

He laughs again, and this time it sounds a little more normal, except that the smile on his face has turned upward sharply. "Oh, that's not what I meant," he says. "I'll buy her, but not for four hundred."

I realize that I've lost a good opportunity by not selling Astrid the last time I was here. At least I could still ask for three hundred, which is the same as I'd gotten for the other three babies. "Okay," I say. "So three hundred then?"

Inwardly, I chastised myself, because I shouldn't have made that sound like a question. When I'm negotiating, I know that I need to sound firm and confident. Hopefully, he accepts the three hundred coin suggestion.

In the corner of my eye, I see the blond man get up and leave the bar, and he looks like he's in a hurry.

But I return my gaze to Max, who is shaking his head. "I'm afraid all bets are off, little lady, since you insulted me before. I'll give you two hundred and not a penny more."

"But... but that's half—"

"One fifty," Max says, cutting me off. "The more you say, the less you get."

"I'll... I'll take it," I say.

"Smart girl," he says. "Now, hand her over to Miss Precious over there, and I'll get you your money. Then you have to get out of here and never come back."

I nod. He doesn't have to tell me that twice.

I collect the money from the bartender, who I guess is on Max's payroll, and leave the bar, trying not to look back at Astrid. I hear her crying as I go, and I have to harden myself not to turn around and grab her away from them.

I guess I'm not a great mom after all, but I'm sure she'll be okay.

I can do a lot with a hundred and fifty gold coins on my own.

MARK

Tristan, Eli, Reece, and I have just met up outside the train station, where Reece has just seen Rose and the babies off to head back to my castle, where she wants to talk to Barbara directly.

"Do any of us think that's a good idea?" asks Eli.

We all look at each other, knowing the answer, but also knowing that we can't keep Rose from doing everything she can to find Trisha.

Reece says it out loud first. "I'm not going to be the one to stop Rose," he says.

"I think we're in agreement then," I say, chuckling lightly until I look at Tristan's face.

It still has the look of pain and horror that all of us felt not long ago when our own children were missing. That look on his face brings it all back to me, and I refocus my determination to find his daughter. Even though Trisha isn't my own child, she's Rose's little girl. And that makes her my priority, too.

"I think it's safe to say that Trisha is out of this city now," says Eli. "So we could split up, or we could keep chasing down leads together."

"I don't have any leads," says Tristan. He barely seems capable of getting the words out of his mouth.

I'm about to open my own mouth to speak when I hear a voice in my head. "Alpha Mark," a man's voice says.

I recognize it instantly as Chester. He's one of the warriors I've sent out to neighboring towns and cities to look for all the babies, and who are now all concentrating on finding Trisha. Chester has a family of his own, and it wasn't that long ago that his wife had a little girl with bright blonde hair and blue eyes, just like his father.

"I think I know where the Alpha can find his daughter," Chester says.

CHAPTER 30: I WILL KILL HIM

TRISTAN

Mark is driving as I sit in the passenger seat, and he is driving us to the Goddess forsaken town that Chester is waiting to meet us in. Chester asked Mark if he wanted him to go in and try to get the baby, which is probably my sweet Trisha, from the man who has just purchased her. Mark deferred to me, and while it was tempting to have him go ahead and try to grab her, I told him to hold off. It was too dangerous, and Mark had just mentioned that Chester had a baby at home, too.

Drumming my fingers on the console, I will Mark to drive faster, even though I know he's already driving as fast as possible. It wouldn't do Trisha any good for us to crash on the way to save her.

We are optimistic. That's why there is a car seat in the back.

"Chester is keeping an eye on the front of the tavern while another of my men, David, has his eyes on the back door," Mark explains to me. There are only two entrances/exits in that place, so if Max goes somewhere, he'll be seen by one of them.

I nod, not trusting my voice to even attempt to speak.

"Also, David's wife, Brenda, who is a vicious she-wolf warrior, is tailing Retta. Apparently, she's got some rundown car she's driving at

147

the moment. She's not sure if she bought it or if she stole it, but she's driving out of town right now," Mark fills me in.

"Is Brenda in a vehicle?" I ask, my voice cracking a little. This is why I didn't want to say anything before.

"Yes, she's following her. Don't worry. She'll make sure that Retta doesn't expect anything. I'm going to have Reece take some warriors out to cut her off and catch her," he explains. "Does that sound like a plan to you?"

"Sure." I turn and stare out the window, waiting until we get close to the town. Then, I know that I will feel dragons swarming my stomach instead of just the butterflies I feel now. Nervous, anxious, vomitous... I'm about to come out of my skin.

Picturing Trisha's little face in my mind fuels the rage I feel inside of me. I can't believe the nerve of this bitch Retta. I want to be the one to trail her so that I can make her wreck her car, shift into my wolf, and completely devour her.

Part of me wants to see her rotting in prison for this, but I also just want to end her life and have the satisfaction of seeing her cold, lifeless eyes staring up at me as her blood coats my paws.

"Here we are," Mark says as I see a city come into view in the distance.

This isn't the little village I was expecting. It's actually quite large. How she was unable to hide in a place like this is remarkable to me.

"Where's Eli?" I manage to ask as I am ready to get out of the car at a stoplight and make a run for it, even though I know that won't be faster.

"I went ahead and told him he could go look for his sister," Mark explains. "I figure we'll have Trisha and Retta in our custody in a matter of minutes, so he may as well go try to find Kelly."

"And Rose is still going back to the castle to face off against Barbara with just Adam and Shelby?" None of us has thought that this is the best idea, but we are not arguing with her about anything at this point.

"That's right," he says. He turns and heads into what is clearly the seedier part of town. We pull into a parking lot of a tavern that has quite a few people traipsing in and out of it now that night has fallen. It seems like it's been a month since I held my baby, but she's not even a week old.

A couple of girls wearing next to nothing catcall us. I turn and glare at them, and they back away. I walk inside, followed by Mark. I need some direction as to where to go, and currently I'm charging in like a bull with absolutely no idea where I'm going, but if anyone comes anywhere near me, I will punch them in the face with no questions asked.

A blond guy comes over to Mark quickly. "He's back there," he says, pointing down a hallway behind the bar. "He took her back there."

"Thank you, Chester," Mark says, patting him on the shoulder. "You will be rewarded for this."

"It is an honor to help, Alpha," Chester says. "I'll wait out here in case he tries to come out this way."

I leap over the bar in one move, and the bartender shouts at me, "Hey, what the fuck do you think you're doing?"

"Whatever the fuck he wants to," Alpha Mark says, coming over the bar behind me.

The bartender must not have seen him until then, but he instantly recognized the Alpha of his land. "Yes, Alpha," he says, bowing his head.

The door is locked, so I kick it in.

"I have a key…." the bartender says, a few moments too late.

I don't even turn around to acknowledge him.

There are three doors in this hallway. I have to choose one, leave one to Mark, and hope the asshole isn't behind the third one. If he is, maybe Chester will stop him. But if this bastard touches my daughter in a painful way, I swear to the Goddess, I will kill him.

We stop behind the first two doors and listen and hear nothing. I move down a little further, and behind the third door, I hear the thumping of heartbeats.

Multiple heartbeats.

One of them sounds larger than the others. Confused, I turn to look at Mark, who is behind me now. He hears it, too. 'What the actual fuck?' I ask him through the mind-link.

He shakes his head at me, and I prepare to kick the door in, hoping none of the children on the other side of the door get hurt. It sounds like there are a lot of them.

I get the door open with one kick, and my eyes can barely register what I am seeing.

The room isn't large, maybe the size of a small bedroom, but in it, there are dozens and dozens of children. The oldest ones look to be about five. They are dirty and wearing rags, and the bigger ones are chained to cots, three or four of them on each one.

In the middle stands a creepy looking man who is glaring at me. He has my daughter in his arms, and I can tell by his expression he will hurt her if I don't act with caution.

Before I opened the door, I wondered why it was so quiet, but now I know.

Every single child has a piece of duct tape over their mouth—even Trisha.

I will kill him.

CHAPTER 31: A SILENT ESCAPE

ELI

I'm so relieved that they've found Trisha. Even though I'm not her father, she's part of our family, and with her missing, we weren't complete. I can't imagine how happy Rose will be when she has all four babies there in her arms.

Mark tells me that they haven't quite gotten Trisha out of there, wherever she is, but I know that nothing is going to stop Tristan from getting his daughter back from whatever asshole is holding her. I almost feel sorry for whoever has her. Nah... they're getting what they deserve.

With Trisha and the other pups safe, it's time for me to focus on Kelly. My warriors have been searching for her this whole time, so I'm headed out to meet with them and see what kind of leads they're following. Turns out, they're pretty far away, which makes sense; Kelly would be calling for me if she were within mind-link range, unless she's being blocked. But that's unlikely because blocking requires an Alpha's abilities. I don't think there are any Alphas left who are stupid enough to try to kidnap my sister.

Trevor had been keeping me updated. Brent, Sean, and Valda are still with him out searching, and I'm happy to know that Eustace is also on the search team. I know he's worried about Heather, who is also missing, and I hope that we find both her and Kelly safe and sound.

It takes a while, but I finally catch up with the team, who are stopped at a highway rest stop.

"Alpha." Trevor greets me first. "I'm happy for you that you've found all the pups."

"Thank you," I say. "I want to get back to Rose, but she's fine for now until we find Kelly. Bring me up to speed."

"We lost her scent a while back, but we know they'd been headed in this general direction," he says. "We must be getting close to where she can mind-link us, but no luck so far."

I nod. "Unless there's an Alpha holding her, but I don't see how that's possible with Kane dead," I say. "Stephen is still a threat, but I don't see that moron having the balls to pull off something like this. And I don't understand the point of taking Kelly, either."

Trevor shook his head. "Me neither," he says.

"It makes no sense, especially with the pups kidnapped at the same time, unless one has nothing to do with the other," I say.

The rest of the team, who have been inside the rest stop getting snacks and water out of the vending machines, greet me as they load up into the vehicles.

"We'll keep heading in that direction," I tell Trevor. "We'll see or hear something about her eventually."

He nods and gives me the sign of respect before getting into his vehicle. I lock up my car and join the other team in their SUV, then we head down the road in the same direction they've determined that Kelly was going.

'Hang on, Sis,' I think to myself. 'We're coming.'

~

KELLY

I'm thanking the Goddess right now that whoever put these people in charge of guarding us really is one of the stupidest people on the planet—either that, or they actually want us to escape.

This is too easy.

Randolph, who was incredibly creepy at first but who is now completely on our side and is actually a nice guy, has managed to get them all drunk and half asleep upstairs. The plan is to walk right by them, which makes me nervous because I don't know how the girls will handle that, but I know this will work.

"Thank you for this, Randolph," I say as he unlocks my chains. He's not supposed to have the keys, but he managed to get them after the main guard passed out and the others were busy. "How did you distract them?" I ask.

His face turns bright red and he sort of looks away. "I... I sort of found them something to watch online," he says, still not looking at me.

I shake my head, because I can imagine what would keep a bunch of rowdy bachelors entertained, and it's probably something of the adult variety. I don't ask him any more questions. As long as it worked, it doesn't matter.

After he unlocks the girls' chains, I bring them both close to me. "Okay," I tell them. "This will be easy; we just have to stay quiet. These guys are passed out drunk right now, so all we have to do is sneak by them, and we'll be fine."

Heather nods and looks determined, but Kara looks terrified. I can only imagine what she's been through, being stuck with these awful male guards all alone for who knows how long. She doesn't even remember what's outside of this bunker, or whatever it is, so it's been a long time since she's been anywhere but here.

I'll take her back to my pack where she can be safe and can live a normal life. Eli will see to that.

We inch up toward the door and I hold the girls behind me while Randolph stays up front. I'll have to take him back to my pack, too, because these guys will kill him for helping us escape. He's really not a bad guy. He just needs some help and some positive influence. I think our pack can give him that.

He stops at the top of the stairway and puts his finger to his lips. I nod—of course, we're going to be quiet right now. Once he's sure they're passed out, he waves us forward, and we tiptoe up the stairs. Heather looks confident, but I can feel Kara shaking as she squeezes my hand tight.

I squeeze back and smile at her in a reassuring way. I'm a little worried that she's going to panic right now and give us away, but we have to do this. I'm not leaving her behind. I put my hand over my mouth to encourage her to do the same, and she does, so she's a little less likely to cry out if something happens.

Randolph gets past the guards, who are all snoozing with their heads down on the table. There's a laptop in front of them that's closed now, and it looks like they'd been playing cards as well. Empty and half-empty bottles of beer and hard liquor are everywhere.

Now it's time to sneak the girls by the snoring guards, and I look back at Kara. I'm not worried about Heather at all now; that girl is tough as nails. Kara still has her hand over her mouth, so I nod at her encouragingly while I gently guide her past the sleeping men.

We're clear of them now and on the other side of the room. Kara looks back one last time. While she does so, her foot catches on a bucket on the floor.

The banging echoes through the room, and we all freeze in place. Heather reaches down to stop it from making more noise while I look nervously at the drunk guards. One of them stirs, moving around and grunting, but he just rearranges his arm and lays right back down on it—he's back to snoring in no time.

I don't dare let out a breath as I move the girls forward, and Randolph goes ahead of us to open the outside door. It's something like a hatch—I have no idea what kind of place this could be—but it's big enough for all of us to pass through one at a time, including Randolph.

It's dusk outside, so the sun isn't bright, which I'm glad for. After all that time underground, I don't think I'd even be able to see in bright sunlight.

There are no guards up top, but I feel exposed because we're in a big open area of some sort. I point toward the tree line, indicating to Randolph to run that way.

Once there, I pause a moment and look back to figure out what kind of a place this is. Just then, a small plane starts heading our way from off in the distance. It's getting lower and closer by the minute, and I realize this is an airport of some sort. It's small, but it definitely has a runway and some buildings, and I see some people off in the distance who thankfully don't seem to have seen us.

"Randolph," I say. "That way, where the sun is setting. That's west. I want you to take the girls and run as fast as you can that way."

"What?" asks Kara, shaking her head. "No. We can't go alone!"

"You're not alone," I say. "Randolph is with you."

"But he's—"

"He's fine," I say. "He just helped us escape. Heather, I want you to look out for Kara."

Heather nods. I know she's been isolated all her life, too, but she has a cool head about her and seems to have a great instinct for survival.

"Why aren't you coming?" asks Kara, a pleading look in her eyes.

"I need to find out what's going on here, and who is behind all this," I say. "When you find someone, tell them to get one of the Alphas—Eli, Mark, Tristan, or Reece—whoever's territory we're closest to. Tell them I'm at an airport, and to send people."

Then I look at Randolph. "I'm trusting you to take care of them," I say.

He nods sharply, then Heather takes Kara by the hand. "Come on," she tells her. "We gotta get outta here."

Kara looks at me one last time then reluctantly goes with them. I wait until I can't see them running through the trees anymore, then I start making my way along the tree line closer to the airport buildings.

I need to know what's going on here.

CHAPTER 32: I'LL TELL YOUR MOTHER

"You give me my baby, and I won't rip you to shreds," I say to the man who is holding Trisha. She can't cry because her mouth is taped closed, but I can see that her face is red, and she has tears streaming down her cheeks. I think she might be having trouble breathing. I need to get to my daughter now.

"You will let me walk out of here, or else the baby gets it," the asshole says back to me with a disturbing smile on his face.

I shake my head. "No. That's absolutely not happening. My daughter and these other kids are not going anywhere with you. I am serious, you fucking bastard. Listen to me right now. I am an Alpha. I can shift and rip your throat out before you have time to squeeze my little girl, so the question on your mind shouldn't be how am I going to get out of here alive. It should be how long am I gonna live. Right now, the answer to that question is less than a minute."

He has the audacity to chuckle at me. "Do you really think I am afraid that you will tackle me and try to take the girl? Don't be ridiculous. You may be fast, but I'm pretty damn quick myself. No, you wouldn't risk it."

"If you so much as touch a hair on her head, I will literally eat your heart while you watch me," I tell him.

Mark intervenes, always the calm voice of reason. "Max, what the fuck are you doing?" he asks, using his Alpha voice. "I'd heard about some shady dealings going on in taverns across the pack lands, but I had no idea it was this. And you're involved? You're in a reputable town. How the hell did you get caught up in this?"

"It was that asshole in Amityville!" he screams at me. "Steven got me into it. He said there's good money in baby trafficking. But once I got my first one...." His eyes go across the room to a little girl who is sitting quietly on a filthy cot. She's probably about four, and she looks awful, like she hasn't had a decent meal in her entire life. "Well, once I got little Delilah over there, I knew I couldn't actually sell my children to anyone."

"These are not your children!" I growl at him. Mark puts his hand on my arm to try to calm me down, but I want to rip it off with my teeth.

"Some of them are," he argues. "Some of them I've adopted. I've gone through the proper channels. Their parents simply didn't want them, so now they are mine."

"All right, Max," Mark says. "We'll sort that all out back at the palace, but for now, give my friend his daughter. Clearly, she is not yours."

His eyes widen and then narrow. "No," he says. "I won't. I like this one. I like her curly black hair."

"You would rather die before we can even talk about the possibility of you getting to keep any of your kids?" Mark asks.

Through the mind-link I ask him, 'Are you insane?'

He doesn't even flicker an eyelash at me. 'I'm just making sure Trisha is safe. No, I'm not going to let him have any of these kids. I'll kill him myself.'

I relax only slightly when I realize Mark is bluffing.

But then, Max seems to know that, too. "You won't let me walk out of here," he says. "No, the fact that I'm holding this baby is the only thing that's keeping me alive."

"That's not true," Mark says, and once again, even I believe him. "Max, we've known each other a long time. Just set the baby down, and you and I will go talk while Alpha Tristan takes care of his daughter."

"He really is an Alpha?" He perks up at the sound of my title. Like he didn't know before. "My new baby is the daughter of an Alpha?"

I cannot help the low growl that emanates from the back of my throat. Mark sends me a reminder through the mind-link that that's not helping.

"Trisha is the daughter of an Alpha," Mark says. "So… hand her over, and you're less inclined to die today." Mark takes a few cautious steps forward, but Max retreats. He can't go far without running into a baby crib full of infants who would be screaming if they could open their mouths. I have to wonder how many children have died in this room, choked to death, starved. Goddess, I hope none.

Mark is slowly walking closer to the asshole, and as he goes, he is using his Alpha tone to make the bastard more compliant, though he is still doing his best to resist.

"It's really simple, Max. I'm gonna take this baby, and you're going to go back to the palace with me to   discuss what happens next. Otherwise, I'm going to have to call Prudence in a bit to tell her that her son is not the man she thinks he is, that he murdered a baby and got ripped to shreds by the little girl's dad. Now, is that what you want your sweet mother to hear me say?"

Immediately the fucker breaks into tears. "Don't tell my mom! Please, don't tell my mom!"

Mark is able to get him to release Trisha to him, and in an instant, I am there taking my daughter from him. I can't help but punch the guy right in the face, though. Blood squirts everywhere, barely missing the babies beside him.

Mark gives me a disapproving look, but he doesn't dare say anything. I have my daughter back in my arms now, but I still need help. I don't want to hurt her by ripping this tape off, and I need a bottle. And a new diaper….

Immediately, a group of guards rushes in to take Max into custody.

As soon as he is out of the room, a flock of women appear. Many of them have the necessities we need for these kids. Diapers, bottles, formula, food.

One of them comes over to me with a cotton ball. "Let's see if we can get that adhesive off so we can feed this little princess, okay?" she says.

I don't want to let go of my daughter, but I hold her out so she can do her magic, and in a few seconds the tape comes off. Trisha starts to cry, and it is the most beautiful sound I've ever heard in my entire life.

'I've got her, Rose,' I tell my little flower through the mind-link. 'Our family is complete again.'

'Thank the Moon Goddess!' she says. 'I'm at the castle now. Getting ready to go downstairs.'

'Please be careful,' I tell her.

'Don't worry. In my current state, no one would mess with me.'

I believe her.

Mark catches my eye. "You okay here?"

I look around the room at the dozens of screaming children. I don't think I'm quite the man for this job, but I nod. "Where are you going?"

"Chester has another gift for us," Mark explains. I arch an eyebrow, and he says one more word that tells me everything I need to know about where he's going. "Retta."

CHAPTE 33: WHY AREN'T YOU HERE?

Eli

"You sure 'bout this, Alpha?" asks Eustace for about the third time.

I'm trying to be patient with him because he wasn't in a real pack with a true Alpha, so he's probably not sure how to act around me. I know we're going to have to deal with the group of shifters that are still living in the abandoned resort up in the hills, but first things first.

I need to find Kelly, and I'm positive we're going in the right direction, because I feel like I'm getting closer to her as we drive.

Our surroundings don't look as promising as my optimism right now, though. The farther we go, the more we seem to be headed toward the middle of nowhere. We're far off the highway now on a dirt road that sort of looks like it's been traveled recently, but it's hard to tell because the soil is packed hard.

On one side of the road is a fairly thick forest, and on the other is a big stretch of wide-open fields that must have once been farmlands. There's an old rusty fence that's falling down about every twenty feet, so it clearly hasn't been useful in decades.

Eustace moves suddenly, in a way that's much more energetic than I've seen him move up until now, and he points his finger toward the tree line.

"She's over there!" he yells, even though he's sitting right next to me in the SUV.

Rubbing my ear, I look out the window in the direction he's pointing and shake my head. "I don't see anything," I say.

"She's answered me!" he says. "Pull... pull over, youngin'!"

Brent, who is driving the car, slows down a bit and glances back at me, clearly confused. I'm not sure whether he's trying to figure out if he's really a youngin' since he's not exactly a teenager, or if he really doesn't know who Eustace is talking to. I give him a light nod to show that he should go ahead and come to a stop so we can figure out what's going on here.

It's at that point when I realize that the "she" Eustace is talking about isn't Kelly. It's Heather.

The car barely comes to a stop when Eustace jumps out and starts running toward the forest. I'm not far behind him; if Heather is here, Kelly must be around here somewhere. I need to find her right away. I start asking for her in the mind-link, not really expecting an answer, when I hear a response.

'Eli, is that you?!'

Relief washes over me as I recognize the voice of my sister. I'd feared the worst for so long but hadn't wanted to admit it. But now I know that she's alive, and wherever she is, whatever she's doing, I will definitely find her and bring her home.

She doesn't say anything else yet, so I figure she's running through the forest headed for us, hopefully along with Heather, the girl missing from Eustace's "pack."

But the group that comes running out of the tree line is something I'd never expected.

There's a man, a huge man; he's obviously an Omega, so he's not big in an intimidating way, but he's just really large. Behind him are two young girls, and Kelly is nowhere to be seen. I recognize one of the girls as Heather, and so does Eustace as he runs to her, slowing down a bit as he passes the man and gazing up at him suspiciously.

I know I've never seen the other girl before, or this man, so I stay back a couple of yards while Eustace greets Heather. She looks dirty and hungry, but not too worse for wear, and she's definitely smiling. That tells me that the man is someone who has helped her, so he probably isn't a threat.

'Did you get Heather?' Kelly asks in the mind-link.

'Yes,' I tell her. 'And two other people. Should I be worried about them?'

'That's Randolph. He's harmless,' she says. 'The girl is Kara, and she's a victim too.'

'A victim of what?' I ask. 'And why aren't you here?'

Kelly is quiet for a moment, and I recognize that as my sister doesn't want to share what she's up to. I've dealt with her enough in my life to know that she's up to something. I take the break in conversation to focus on what Eustace and Heather are saying. Heather is introducing the others—Randolph and Kara—and saying that they both helped her escape.

"Where's Kelly?" I ask Heather, hoping I'll get a straight answer out of her since Kelly is still quiet.

"She wanted to explore the airport and see what's going on there," Heather says.

"Airport...."

"The bunker was at the airport," the man—Randolph—explains to me.

I glance over and look him in the eye. He doesn't look afraid of me, but he doesn't look guilty or deceitful either. Since Kelly has already said he is trustworthy, I confine my questions to Kelly's immediate situation. I can find out more about this guy later. "So why did Kelly want to explore it?" I ask.

"She wanted to find out who was in charge there," says the other girl, Kara. "I didn't want her to stay, but she wouldn't listen to me."

I can't help but chuckle. That's Kelly, all right. Once she's made her mind up to do something, there's no talking her out of it.

"Okay," I say. "So where is this airport?"

"We got a little turned around in the forest, so I'm not sure," says Kara.

I look over at Trevor, who's pulling up a map of the area on his phone. "Down this road," he says. "Looks to be a bit south of us."

I nod. "Brent, get these three back to Alpha Mark's castle. It's the closest. I'll inform him and have him get everything ready." I look over at Randolph and the two girls. "You all look like you could use a good meal and a bath. And we have some snacks in the vehicle."

"Thank you," says Heather with a huge smile.

I shudder to think of what has happened to that girl since they've been captured. I'm also worried about Kelly, who has gone silent again, which is odd for her.

Eustace looks at me, and I tell him, "Go with Heather. She'll need you there to get settled. When I get back, we'll talk about what's going on up at your resort and see what we can do to help everyone there."

"'Preciate it, Alpha," he says, then he puts his arm around Heather and leads her to the SUV, where Brent has opened the door for them. The girls and Eustace get in, followed by Randolph.

"Well, let's go get my sister," I say to everyone else, and then I get into the other SUV with Trevor, Sean, and Valda.

As we're driving, I hear from Kelly again. 'I see six people here, and they're talking.'

'Are you somewhere safe?' I ask. 'Kelly, we're almost there. The others are safe and headed back to Mark's castle. Don't do anything stupid.'

'You always were a worry wart, brother,' she says with a hint of a laugh in her voice. 'I'm not going to get caught.'

'All right,' I say. 'We're about ten minutes out.'

I look out at the road and watch the rusty fence pass us as Trevor accelerates. I send a quick message to Mark explaining about the people on their way, and he tells me he'll have his people take care of them. I also tell him to tell Rose that I'll be home as soon as I can. I can't wait to see her there, all happy with all four pups in her arms again.

I have so many questions. I'm sure I'll get answers for a few when I can talk to Kelly more, but wondering who is behind all of this—and why—is giving me a nagging feeling in the pit of my stomach. Why would they want Kelly? It just doesn't make any sense.

We round a corner, and I can finally see the airport off in the distance. It's very small and clearly designed for small planes, so it's not quite what I'd pictured. Since there's so much farmland out here, it's probably where all the small crop-dusting planes land. As we get closer, I see a couple of cars in front of a small building that must house the staff here, although I doubt it takes many people to run this airport.

Now I have even more questions. Where did they keep Kelly and the girls out here? The buildings look small, but they could have some sort of basement where they held them; the one girl, Kara, doesn't look like she's been out in the sunshine in years.

I'm debating whether I should just barge in on what's happening or sneak around to wherever Kelly is hiding.

'I'm here,' I tell her in the mind-link. 'Where are you, and do you want to stay hidden?'

'Yes, definitely,' she says. 'I'm overhearing some good stuff here.'

"Pull into this bushy area here," I tell Trevor.

He does so, and we all get out, quietly. The tree line works its way around the airport, so we'll be able to get in close and probably hide wherever Kelly is at.

'What kind of good stuff?' I ask Kelly.

'Well, I know who's behind all these kidnappings now,' she says.

CHAPTER 34: A PRIZE

ROSE

The second that I hear that Tristan is on his way back to the castle with Trisha, I can breathe again.

All four of my babies are safe and will soon be in my arms. I thank the Moon Goddess repeatedly as I make my way through the halls of the castle to the dungeon.

The guards look concerned as I pass them at the top of the stairs, the bottom of the stairs, and right outside of Barbara's cell door, but they do not speak to me, other than to give me a few words of respect

I nod my head at them, but I am concentrating.

All the way back to Mark's castle from the train station, I have been rehearsing what I want to say to her, how I will confront her, the woman who arranged for my babies to be taken.

If Retta is captured, I will deal with her separately. My understanding is that Mark is in the process of taking her into custody right now.

Both of these women are going to rot in the dungeon for the rest of their lives. But for now, I will be telling Barbara what I think about her.

The cell is dimly lit. Only the light from one lantern casts shadows along the walls and floor. Barbara is sitting in the back of the cell, her arms wrapped around her knees as she stares at the ground.

I wait, staring at her, willing her to glance up. I hope that the light is sufficient enough that she can see me when she does.

It takes a while. She seems to be lost in her own thoughts. When she lifts her head and looks into my eyes, I see a flicker of fear.

But then she smiles at me.

"Well, if it isn't the horrible mother who can't even keep track of her own damn brats," she spits at me with venom.

Fire flickers within my veins. She actually dares to call me out when I'm here to rip her head off.

"I want an explanation, and I want it now," I say to her. "Why the hell would you do something like this?"

She laughs an evil cackle. "Because... you deserved it," she tells me. She has a streak of blood on her face, and I see more on her clothes. Her head has a large welt, right in the middle of her forehead, and I have to think that she was injured in the car wreck.

I'm glad she's hurt. I hope that she lay there and suffered for a really long time. I hope that she is still in pain.

But I'm glad she didn't die.

The chances that I am about to take a life for the first time are pretty high right now, and I don't regret a single murderous thought that is bouncing through my head.

"I deserved it?" I repeat. "Why did I deserve it? Because I was lucky enough to find four wonderful men who love me? Because I have four beautiful children and your child died? Because no one will ever love you because you are a pathetic bitch who is evil to the core? No, Barbara, I didn't deserve for you to fuck around with my life and take my children. And I didn't deserve for you to put my children's lives in danger. But you deserve every tiny fragment of hell that you have coming to you."

She laughs. "You're so wrong, you stupid bitch. King Gene knows where I am. He's already sending people over to the castle to get me out. I'll be released soon, and then, you'll have to watch your back.

You'll never know when I'll be coming for your children or your men."

Now, it is my time to laugh. "King Gene was here," I tell her, watching the smile on her face waver slightly as she realizes I have used the past tense. "He sat upstairs for a long time, preparing to see you. That's when Mark's people told him you were no longer here, that you were in Tristan's castle dungeon. So… he's on his way there now. But what King Gene doesn't know, and is now out of mind-link range for you or anyone else to tell him, is that he's just waltzed right into the middle of a coup."

"What?" Barbara screeches, throwing her hands down on the floor next to her hips. "No, that's not possible. He's on his way here to get me out."

"He's on his way to a very similar situation that you're in, Barbara. He'll be in prison himself soon, and then… well, who will there be to help either of you?" I answer the question for her. "No one."

"You bitch!" she screams at me, but now it is my turn to laugh.

I rarely shift. In fact, I haven't shifted since before I came to live at King Gene's castle. But now is the perfect time to let my wolf out. "Unlock the doors," I tell the guards.

They don't hesitate to do what I say. Maybe there's something to be said for speaking with authority.

Once the gate is open, I leap inside, shifting in midair. My clothes shred and fall away, and I am on top of Barbara before she can even blink.

She's not chained up, and there's no silver or anything to keep her from shifting. She's just too damn slow.

My wolf teeth clamp down on her shoulder first. I bite down hard, ripping into her flesh as the taste of her blood fills my mouth. She screams and tries to hit me, but her human hand feels like a child's as she drums against me.

I haven't decided exactly what I want to do to her yet, but since her hand is beginning to annoy me, like a fly that just won't stop buzzing around my head, I let go of her shoulder and clamp down on her arm around the elbow.

My teeth sink through the flesh as she screams and curses and tries to yank away from me. I crush bone, mangle tendons, shred muscle.

"Oh, Goddess! Fuck! Stop!" Barbara screams.

I do as she asks. I don't like the taste of blood, and I feel like she's gotten enough of what she deserves that I'm finished with her.

Leaving her screaming behind me, I pull away and head back out of the dungeon. I don't bother to shift, but I hear the guards locking up the cell while they call for a healer. She'll need one. She's bleeding profusely.

I trot up the dungeon steps, knowing I'll need a bath. There's blood all down my light yellow fur. I realize then that I'm dripping it all over the floor. I hate to make a mess for the maids, but it can't be helped. There's nothing I can do about it now.

Except for maybe dropping what I'm carrying, but it sort of feels like a prize right now, a reminder of what she's done. For the rest of Barbara's miserable life, she'll know that she didn't get away with stealing my children.

But I will get away with what I took from her.

I continue down the hallway toward my room, getting lots of frightened stares from the staff that I pass with my bloody fur and what I have in my mouth.

A human arm.

CHAPTER 35: A WHOLE NEW LIFE

Kelly

Eli warns me in the mind-link that he's getting close. I brace myself so I won't startle and make noise, and when he moves in behind me, ducking down behind the airport's front desk with me, I nod without looking back at him. I'm too focused on the conversation in front of me.

"When do we get paid?" demands the guy whose name I'd deduced was Ralph, his mouth turned down in a frown.

"I dunno," says Jim, the other guy I'd been watching. "King Gene said we had to keep 'em for a while longer."

"How much longer?" Ralph asks. "I got bills to pay."

"And I don't?" asks Jim. "Just shut up and do your job, and the payout will be so much that you'll never worry about money again."

Apparently, that's enough for Eli, who has called in the others and now stands up confidently and walks across the room. Ralph and Jim freeze; it's obvious that Eli is a powerful Alpha, and they know they're done for.

"Yeah, you won't be mind-linking anyone for a long time," says Eli. I guess he's blocked them from reaching out to Gene.

Eli nods at Trevor, who leads the frightened shifters off without even requiring handcuffs. They look positively terrified. They should be.

"I kind of feel sorry for them," I say half-heartedly.

"Yeah, because kidnapping you is such an innocent thing to do," Eli says with a scowl. "Are you okay?"

"Of course, I am," I say. "I just wanted to find out what the hell is going on here. I still don't know, other than realizing that Gene is involved."

Eli nods. "We'll get a lot more information out of them back at the castle," he says. "Is there anyone else here we should worry about?"

"There were some guards down below, but they're all passed out. You can probably just bring out a team to collect them," I say.

"The team is already on its way," he says. "Down below?"

I nod, pointing out into the general area of the airstrip. "There's some sort of an underground bunker out there where they held us," I say. "And something weird is going on around here. They've held that girl, Kara, down there for years. Is she okay?"

"As good as she can be," he says. "Let's get the hell out of here."

By the time we get outside, other vehicles have arrived, and I show everyone the bunker entrance. Trevor loads Jim and Ralph into an SUV and assigns some guards to watch them while directing a team to get into the bunker.

Eli and I get into another SUV and take off, leaving the teams to deal with the criminal element.

"And I don't even get a hug," I say, winking at Eli. I know he's mad at me for going back to find out what's going on.

He just shakes his head and looks at the road ahead.

Rose

I can't stop crying. First Tristan comes in with Trisha, and my heart feels whole again. I hold my beautiful baby in my arms and feed her while Tristan sits beside us, one arm wrapped around my shoulder and the other stroking little Trisha's beautiful curly locks.

We've barely gotten settled when Reece comes in, and he lifts little Reeva into his arms. Tristan cradles Trisha on his shoulder to burp her, then stands up so Reece can have his seat while he lightly bounces Trisha across the room.

I giggle through my happy tears. It's such a beautiful sight to watch such a strong, powerful Alpha be so gentle and caring.

"I'm so glad to see that look on your face, darlin'," says Reece, gently handing Reeva over to me for her feeding. "You look positively glowing, like the Goddess herself."

"Shh," I say. "I'm no goddess, and I don't want to make her mad now. She's given me so much, and I'm so grateful to her."

"So are we," Tristan whispers from the corner of the room as little Trisha falls asleep in his arms.

Mark walks in the door smiling. "Now, here's a sight I've waited too long to see," he says.

Tristan immediately shushes him with furrowed eyebrows, then lightly bounces Trisha a little more.

"After all that little girl has been through," I tell him, "I'm sure she can sleep through anything."

Tristan laughs a little and sets Trisha down in her little bassinet just as little Reeva has decided she's already had enough to eat. It's a challenge to keep four little babies happy, but I wouldn't trade one second of it for anything in the world.

"I'm so happy that Kelly is fine," I say. "I feel horrible that we let her rot in that hole while we had to find the babies."

"I'm sure she completely understands, darlin'," says Reece. "She knew that these little ones needed us first."

"I suppose," I say. "But I still feel bad about making her wait."

"I guess she's made a couple of new friends," says Mark.

"I'm excited to meet them," I say. "And I'm so sorry about the mess I made for the maids. You've told them I've apologized, right?"

Mark chuckles. "Don't worry, baby," he says. "When I told them what you did, they all volunteered to have the honor of cleaning up after the, and I quote, 'badass future Luna.'"

All of us laughed at that. I still can't believe that was actually me who took revenge on Barbara, but I guess I'm stronger than I've ever known I could be, especially when someone messes with my babies. Retta is in the dungeon now, and no doubt she's heard what I did to Barbara. I'm going to let her stew on that for a bit before I pay her a visit.

I've got more important things to take care of first—my beautiful babies and my wonderful Alphas.

A moment later, the gravity of all of it sinks in. "Future Luna," I say, and I let out a breath at the thought of it. It's all a bit overwhelming. As the daughter of an Alpha like my dad, I'd never imagined that much would come from my life other than scrubbing sewers and doing everyone else's dirty work. But here I am, with so many blessings from the Moon Goddess surrounding me.

There was only one thing missing, and I barely had the thought in my mind before he walked in the door.

Eli.

I smile wide and he matches it as he approaches, his beautiful red hair glistening in the soft lighting of the nursery. I'm still so mad that those awful people shaved little Ethan's head. It was so sweet how he matched his dad! I hope it all grows back very soon.

Eli walks around to the other side of the glider chair and gives me a soft kiss, being careful to not disturb little Matthew, who's currently taking his turn at feeding. Eli then walks over and scoops up little Ethan, who has just woken up with all the commotion.

"Where's Kelly?" I ask.

"She's a little... dirty," Eli says. "She wants to make sure her new friends are settled and then take a quick shower before coming to see the pups. You know she'll want to hold every one of them."

"I can't believe she hasn't met them yet!" I say. "So much has happened in so little time."

~

KELLY'S EYES sparkle as she walks into the room. She looks fantastic, without a single scratch on her, but I know she's been through so much.

I'm holding Matthew at the time, so he's the first little one to make her acquaintance.

"He's the most beautiful thing I've ever seen!" she says, taking him gently into her arms.

"They're all so beautiful," I say. "I can't believe how lucky I am."

Reece hands me a tissue, about the hundredth one I've gone through since all my Alphas have gathered around me.

Kelly coos at Matthew while she walks around to the bassinets to meet the other babies. As she stops by each one, their fathers introduce them.

"They're all so incredibly perfect," she says, handing Matthew to Mark so she can hold Ethan. "Come to Auntie Kelly!" she half-whispers. "Where the hell is his red hair?"

We proceed to tell her the story of those criminals who stole him, and I can see that she hugs him a little tighter.

The door cracks open, and Shelby walks in saying, "Now, why are we having a party without inviting Aunt Shelby and Uncle Adam?"

Adam comes in right behind her. The nearest baby is Trisha, and Tristan reluctantly hands her over so Shelby can cradle her in the corner rocking chair.

I look around at my huge new family and the tears start falling again.

"Darlin'," says Reece, "I'm going to need to get you a new case of tissues."

I laugh, and so does everyone else. "I can't help it," I say. "I just... I just can't say how happy I am right now."

"So are we, little flower," says Tristan. "So are we."

I take another look around the room at my beautiful children, my handsome Alphas, and my good friends, who have become a solid, supportive family for me.

I know that there's nothing that can happen to any of us that can ever keep us from being together. I'm blessed by the Moon Goddess in more ways than I can count, and I'm so excited for the future of my family.

Being a Breeder to four alphas has changed my life... forever.

CHAPTER 36: UNFINISHED BUSINESS

MARK

It's been a couple of days, but I still can't quite shake the nerves. The pups are back and safe in my beautiful Rose's arms. Kelly is back and brought with her another young girl who needs our protection. Rose is safe and well-protected in my castle. All the other Alphas and I are fine.

It sounds like a perfect situation, but I'm restless because we have unfinished business. Gene is still out there somewhere, and I won't feel like everyone is truly safe until we take care of him. Obviously, his mental capacity is diminished, which I think makes him more dangerous. That's why people like Barbara were able to get him to do their dirty work.

Thankfully, I'm not worried about Barbara anymore. When my beautiful Rose told me how she took care of her, I had to smile. She has really transformed from that shy and nervous woman who first arrived at the castle for the contest. Now, she's a confident mother who knows how to defend herself and her pups. I'm so proud of her. Barbara will be locked up for the rest of her life now… missing an arm.

I know that the rest of the Alphas have the same nervous energy, and that's why we're going to get together today and talk about our next move. I've got a few ideas about that.

My mind is filled with thoughts about our next move as I run into Kelly heading down the hall toward Rose's room. We lockstep as we're headed in the same direction.

"Hey," she says. "I hear I'm on duty for a bit."

I nod. "Yes. The other Alphas and I need to regroup. If you and Shelby can spend time with Rose and the pups, that would be great."

"Of course," she says. "And if you need someone to tear Gene's eyeballs out, I'm your gal."

I laugh. "I'll keep that in mind, though I think you have some plans of your own to keep you busy, right?"

"Yes, I'm taking Heather back to the resort," she says. "But I'm going to wait until you Alphas deal with Gene first. I'm not taking Rose and those pups out of my sight until I know he's under control."

"I appreciate that… we all do, Kelly," I say.

She smiles.

"Hey, how are you doing?" I ask. "You've gone through quite a bit yourself lately."

She gives me a crooked smile and waves off my question. "Eh, that's nothing compared to what Rose and the pups went through. I'm fine."

"Good to hear," I say.

We arrive at Rose's room and open the door quietly. I don't want to disturb any of the pups, or Rose, if she happens to be napping. I can't even imagine what it must take to feed four pups at once. I know I'd be exhausted.

But she's awake, and I see her beautiful eyes twinkle as she spots me. I can spot my little Matthew from a mile away, and right now, he happens to be the one getting breakfast from his mom. I want to hold both of them, but for now, I'm content with a gentle kiss on Rose's lips and a stroke on my little boy's head.

"How did you sleep?" I ask.

It was Tristan's night to be with Rose, and he's standing in the corner bouncing his little girl with love in his eyes. We're taking turns spending the night with Rose again, though with her being so busy with the babies, our nights with her are more like baby duty, and let me tell you, not one of us Alphas are complaining. Compared to what we faced over these past weeks, changing a diaper is heaven.

"I don't know that I ever sleep." She giggles, and I know she's not complaining at all.

"Well, try to rest sometimes anyway, beautiful," I say.

"Oh, I do," she says. "It's just hard to fall asleep and miss one second of time with them."

The way she looks at our son makes me smile. I give her another kiss and savor the flavor of her lips.

"My turn," says Tristan.

Suddenly, he's right behind me, and I look back and see that baby Trisha is back snuggled in her crib, fast asleep. I laugh and step aside for him to have his moment with Rose before we head to the council room of my castle to meet with the others.

I smile one more time at the beautiful sight of Rose and my son nestled comfortably in an overstuffed chair and head out the door with Tristan just as Shelby arrives.

We greet her before she goes in, then we walk for a few steps in silence before he says, "Damn, this is all so surreal."

I nod. "I can't believe it either. I don't think it's possible to thank the Moon Goddess enough for how things turned out."

"I hear that," he says.

It doesn't take long to get to the council room, where Reece and Eli are already waiting for us. They look a little impatient, and I don't blame them. All that nervous energy is coming back to me. I guess Rose had been a temporary cure.

"It's about time you got here," says Eli. "So, where do we go to kill the bastard?"

"Oh, come on, Eli," says Tristan with a laugh. "Tell us how you really feel."

I chuckle lightly and pour a cup of coffee from the station the servants left in the corner. "As with the rest of you, I've got scouts everywhere. He won't hide for long."

"I haven't heard from any of my people yet," says Reece. "But let me tell you, they're all so angry they're ready to tear him limb from limb when they find him. I had to give my Alphas commands that they leave him for us. They agreed of course, but they're not happy."

Eli nodded. "That bastard has caused a lot of death and heartache. The worst part is that none of that needed to happen. He's the dumbass who thought up the contest in the first place. He decides not to keep his word, then suddenly our people have to pay the price."

"I think this whole thing calls for a public punishment," I say. "As much as we want to just take care of him right away ourselves, I think the whole kingdom has the right to see justice done."

Reece nods. "I agree there. I think it'll do the kingdom good."

I open my mouth to add something, but the door opens, and a couple of servants walk in with two huge trays of pastries. We've got one of the best pastry chefs in the world here, so my mouth starts watering from the scent immediately.

Tristan is the first to reach for one and practically shoves the whole thing in his mouth. He looks up and we're all just staring at him.

"What?" he asks, his mouth half full. "I can't help it the food here is delicious."

I laugh and thank the servants, who walk out of the room with a giggle. I take a pastry myself, and we have a few minutes where we're doing nothing but eating. Frankly, I think we need it. It was hard to stomach anything when the pups were missing, so we have some catching up to do in the eating department. Besides, we need to shovel it in before Tristan downs all of it.

Thankfully, the servants left some towels to clean up because I need to handle the kingdom map so we can get down to business. The other Alphas move the empty trays aside and I spread it out on the big conference table.

"All right, we've got all four directions covered, so that's good," I say.

In this situation, it's a damn good thing that there are four of us.

"Does anyone have any ideas of where he'd hide?" I ask. "Who knows Gene the best?"

We all just look at each other.

Reece shakes his head. "My parents knew his father, but honestly, I'd never stepped foot in the Dark Forest castle before the contest."

"Same," says Eli. "It's like that bastard kept himself secluded because he knew he didn't deserve the crown."

"I'm sure that's the case," I agreed. "Tristan?"

Tristan shrugs and pours himself another cup of coffee. "Nope, just met the guy myself."

"Well, we have nothing to work with on that end," I say. "Maybe Adam knows something that can help. Let's get him in here."

I mind-link with Adam. "All right, he'll be here," I say. "In the meantime, let's think about Gene's punishment. I'm sure we'll get word from our warriors as soon as they find him."

"Nothing short of hanging works for me," Eli says. The look in his eyes says he's definitely had enough. I don't blame him. His sister got kidnapped as well as his baby, so he's been through a lot.

"I don't know, that may be too quick," says Reece. "If we lock him in the dungeon forever, he's not a threat. I think he's too stupid to be dangerous."

I nod and start to chime in, but Tristan's voice rings out from the corner by the coffee station.

"I have a better idea."

We all turn to him, and he's got a huge smirk on his face. Oh, boy.

CHAPTER 37: WE HAVE A PLAN

Having Kelly and Shelby with me while I feed the babies is so wonderful. It's so hard for me to believe that just a few days ago, Kelly was missing–and so were my babies. I've been kidnapped myself, and I know how awful it is. I hate that anyone else has had to go through that. I thank the Moon Goddess several times a day that we are all safe and together again now.

"Which baby do you think looks the most like his or her daddy?" Shelby asks. She is holding baby Matthew, cooing at him while I hold both girls. While both of the women in the room are aunties to all four of my children, Kelly can hardly let go of her actual nephew, Ethan, whom she is holding now.

"Well, I'm super upset that I didn't get to see the red curls on this one," she begins, speaking in a baby voice as if Ethan can understand her. He is cooing, so maybe he can–to a point. "But I still think he has his daddy's nose."

"He does," I agree, smiling over at them. "Tricia definitely has her daddy's hair, but Reeva has her father's mouth."

"They are all so cute," Shelby says, and I think I hear a note of

183

longing in her voice. It might not be long until she starts asking Adam if they can start trying.

"What are your plans for the people who you collected along your journey?" Shelby asks Kelly. I'm curious, too. I've met the girls, and they are both gems. I was a little bit alarmed when I met some of the other characters, especially Eustace, but he's a sweet guy.

"I promised to help the folks back at the hotel," Kelly explains. "Their land isn't quite in Alpha King Gene's territory, but it's close enough that we could probably annex it once we get this all sorted out."

"All sorted out," Shelby mutters under her breath, and I know what she's thinking. It will take a lot of sorting.

"Where is Gene?" I ask, refusing to call him king any longer. He's messed with my family long enough. It's hard to believe that he's not behind all of the attempts on my life, my children's lives, and the Alphas.

"I'm not sure." Kelly looks over her shoulder toward the door. The Alphas have been gone for a while, and I wonder if they're not discussing just that. "But I think we can rest assured he's not going to just skate by."

Sure enough, only a moment after she finishes her sentence, the door opens, and my men walk in. I smile. Looking at all of their handsome faces makes me so happy. Tristan is leading the pack, and that tells me there's something they want to say. I take a deep breath and arch an eyebrow.

"Guess what, my little flower," he begins, clasping his massive hands together. "We have a plan."

"Oh, no," I mutter, shaking my head. "Why can I already tell that this is something I'm not going to like?"

"Because it's Tristan talking," Mark says with a wry grin.

"Hey now," Tristan begins.

"He's not wrong," I point out. "What's your plan, Tristan?"

He claps his hands together again, and his daughter stirs. I motion for him to be quiet and he apologizes in a whisper. "Sorry! Sorry!

Okay, here's the deal. We're gonna track Gene down and make him pay for being a despicable asshole."

I pause for a moment, waiting for him to continue. He doesn't. I shift my gaze to Eli, then Reece, who are also looking at me wide eyed. By the time I get to Mark, he is able to give me a small shrug, like he doesn't know what Tristan's doing either.

I return my gaze to Tristan. "What?"

"Yeah. We're gonna make him pay."

"Okay, but how?" I ask. "When? Do you have any idea where he is?"

"We know he's not back at his castle," Reece offers with another shrug.

"Oh, good. Then that just leaves literally every place else in the world for you to look." I roll my eyes, not thinking this is the best put together plan.

"It won't take us long to sniff him out." Tristan sounds confident, and he had no reason not to. All four of my Alphas are competent. They are strong, intelligent, and very good at everything they do. If they put their minds to something, I have no doubt, they will accomplish it.

Especially when it's someone like Gene they are trying to track down. He is the most incompetent person I've ever met in my life. It's hard to believe that he was ever chosen to be king. Why, it was his own incompetence that led him here in the first place. Where he ever got this hair-brained notion that he could bring these four Alphas in to have a contest to find someone to take over the throne, I have no idea. I wonder now, though, if maybe Emily didn't put him up to it. She did want to be queen awfully bad. It's the only thing that makes sense to me.

"Rose?" Reece saying my name snaps me out of my thoughts. "Are you okay?"

"Yeah, I'm fine." I blink a few times, wondering if I haven't been falling asleep. With four babies, Mama doesn't get a lot of time to rest, even with half the castle wanting to help. I'm the only one who can feed these little pups after all. "Are you planning on going now?" Fear bubbles up inside of me as I think about all we've been through. I don't want to lose anyone again.

"We need to get this over with," Mark says, reluctantly. "But don't worry. You'll be safe here. We've got all of our armies still on standby."

"I've heard that one before," I mutter.

"It's true this time," Eli assures me.

"What about you guys?" Shelby asks. "Won't you need your own troops to go along with you?"

Tristan shakes his head. "Not many. We'll take a few, but from what we've heard, after the last few battles we've won, no one will be standing up against us. Everyone is afraid of us."

"As they should be," Reece adds. All of them look proud, and they should. They've done a good job of destroying our enemies.

But I'm still nervous. "You have to be careful. Gene is a lunatic. You never know what he might do."

"We will be careful," Tristan promises me, and the others nod in agreement.

"Are you going to kill him?" Kelly asks. "Because he deserves to die."

A crooked grin forms on Tristan's handsome face. "Nope. We have something else in mind."

"What is that?" I ask, tipping my head to the side and looking at him with one eye.

"You'll see." Tristan rumbles with a chuckle, and the other Alphas join in as well.

"I'm not sure that I like the sound of that either," I mutter, but I don't have any choice in the matter. "Who will be king if you don't kill Gene?"

"We'll force him to abdicate, and then we'll all take over," Eli explains.

"Don't worry. We've got the territories all worked out," Reece adds. "We'll all rule our area, with you as Luna Queen over it all."

Again, I'm caught off guard. "Me?" I ask. "Luna Queen?"

"Who else?" Mark flashes me a dazzling smile, and I feel heat rise in my face.

I think back to where I started, how my parents didn't even love me, how I was cleaning up shit in another kingdom. Now, I am with the four most amazing men. I have four beautiful babies. And I'm about to be the Luna Queen of the entire kingdom.

It seems unreal.

"Thank the Goddess for my magical uterine horns," I murmur.

"What's that?" Tristan asks.

"Nothing." I shake my head to clear it. I know I can't talk them out of it, so I don't bother to try. "Be careful."

"Always," Tristan says, raising a hand as if he's giving an oath. One by one, my men step over to lean down and kiss me without disturbing the sleeping princesses. And that's what they are, too. Princesses.

I take a moment to enjoy the feel of each of my Alphas' mouths against mine, and when they are done, I tell them each that I love them and send them out into the world. I have no idea what they're going to do when they're gone, but I pray to the Moon Goddess they'll all come back safely this time–and no one will be kidnapped!

CHAPTER 38: LOOSE ENDS

ELI

I'm still not sure what to think of Tristan's idea, but the rest of the Alphas seem to want to run with it. Personally, I'd rather see Gene's head strung up on a pole, but I guess since we're all going to be running a kingdom together, we need to compromise. I suppose I'll see how I feel about it when we finally catch the bastard.

It doesn't seem like that's happening very soon. We're being pulled in different directions, all for dead ends. Right now, we're following up a lead of some guy with a long beard in Mark's territory who's been holed up in a shack on some agricultural land. Apparently, the owner saw him and thought he was suspicious, so he reported it to Mark's warriors.

Gene didn't have a beard when I saw him last, and it's a pretty cheesy way to disguise himself, if not just flat-out stupid, so I suppose it could actually be him. He's not exactly the brightest bulb.

We're at the main house on the property talking to the owner, a man who is ironically also named Mark. This Mark is whispering to Alpha Mark about the guy on his land.

"He showed up a few days ago," Mark the farmer says. "He didn't ask if he could stay there, and I've been noticing produce gone from my storehouse, lots of it. The guy eats like a two-ton bull. I can't afford to feed some guy who doesn't even work for me."

Alpha Mark nods. "Don't worry. We'll take care of it."

The farmer nods back and quickly retreats into his house. I guess he doesn't want to see what happens next. Maybe he thinks that if it is Gene, we'll slaughter him right here. I can't say he's wrong. At least, that's what I want to do.

But I'll keep that to myself for now.

We head off in the direction that Mark the farmer gave us and sure enough, there was a little shack out on the outskirts of his fields. It's out in the middle of nowhere with no trees for cover, so we collectively decide after a quick mind-link meeting that we're just going to march right out there. This guy is no match for four powerful Alphas, after all.

The entrance is on the opposite side of our approach, so we're hoping he doesn't spot us in the window and try to run. I'm in no mood to run, and if it's Gene, I can't promise he won't accidentally get a wolf jaw to the neck.

But as we get closer, it looks like there won't be a chase at all. As we round the corner and see the shack entrance, we spot the guy with the beard sitting there drinking a cup of what looks like coffee but smells awful just sitting on the board that's serving as the front porch of the run-down house.

"Aw, I din't know I was gettin' visitors," the man says.

I squint, trying to see if it's Gene, but I can't tell. And I can't get a whiff of his scent because whatever is in that cup smells so awful, I don't even want to try.

But then the guy stands up, and we have before us a lanky guy who's taller than all of us. Nope, this isn't Gene for sure. I try to calm my nerves so I don't yell at the guy for making us come all the way out here.

"Hey, ain't you Alpha Mark?" he asks.

"Yes, I am," Mark says. "I hear you've been causing problems for the landowner here."

"Oh, I ain't mean to cause no trouble, Alpha sir," the guy says.

He certainly sounds sincere. I'm ready to just get out of here and leave him to his boiled mud, or whatever it is he's drinking. We have a rogue ex-king to catch.

"I'm sure you don't, but unfortunately, the farmer is having some problems with missing food," Mark explained, calmer than I would have been able to if these were my pack lands. "Why don't you come with us, and we'll get this all straightened out?"

I sigh, unable to believe that we were going to waste even more time dealing with this, but then I force myself to calm down. These are Mark's pack lands, and he needs to help the people who live in them. I follow them and the other Alphas, who haven't said a word but look a tad annoyed as well, back to Farmer Mark's house.

"That's him!" the farmer yells. He's finally brave enough to come outside because we didn't fight anybody, I guess.

"All right, what's your name, sir?" Alpha Mark politely asks the guy.

"Smithy," he says.

"Okay, Smithy, did you steal food from this man's storage unit?" Mark asks.

Smithy looks at the farmer, and there's guilt all over his face. Finally, he admits he did it and apologizes, and Mark works out something with Farmer Mark so this guy could do some work for him and earn regular meals. Apparently, the farmer needed the help anyway. Everyone seems happy with the arrangement, so we finally get to leave.

We all check in with our teams as we're heading back to Mark's castle, which we're not doing very quickly since we might have to go off in another direction at any time now. I really miss Rose and my little Ethan, but I know we need to get this done so we can stop worrying about loose ends. And Gene is the loosest of all ends, that's for sure.

My thoughts freeze when I get a mind-link from one of my warriors on the south part of my territory.

'Alpha Eli, sir, there's something you need to look into out here.'

'What is it?' I ask in the mind-link.

'Well, there's a nice house here, and I'm not sure who these people are, but something is fishy here, that's for sure.'

'Can you give me something more solid than fishy?' I ask.

'Sorry, Alpha, yes,' he says. 'There's a short guy who looks a lot like King... a lot like Gene, and he's been staying here a few days.'

He goes on to describe him more, and the more I hear, the more I know we've got him. I quickly tell the other Alphas, and the driver turns immediately toward the south of my territory. I ask more questions as we drive, and my warrior affirms that he won't let the little weasel go anywhere. He uses that very term, and I have to laugh.

"What's up?" Tristan asks. "I'm supposed to be the funny one, you know."

I shake my head and smile. "It's nothing. I'm just positive this is our rat. We've finally flushed him out."

I'm glad we've found him, but I'm even happier to know that this is almost over, and I can just spend all my time—at least, my allotted time since we're splitting nights with Rose—with the love of my life and our tiny little son. I just want us all to be a family again, together, without any worries about kidnappings or anything else.

It's quite a haul to my territory, especially to the south end, but Mark's driver makes good time and we're there fairly quickly. We head straight to the house in question and meet up with my warrior, James.

"He's inside," James says. "I have guys watching all the exits and even a few places that aren't exits, and he's definitely still in there."

I nod. "Thank you, James. Please keep a look out while we approach. If anyone tries to run, catch him, but leave him for us."

"Yes, Alpha," James says, then he gives me the sign of respect.

Tristan, Mark, Reece, and I walk right up to the front door and knock. Once again, we know there's no one inside who would stand a chance against the four of us.

The door creaks open lightly, and a young maid asks, "Who's there?"

"It's Alpha Eli," I say firmly. "Let us in."

"I-I have to check with the master of the house first."

192

I just look at her. She knows she has to do as I say, so it doesn't take much more than that for her to open the door the rest of the way.

"What's the meaning of this?" a man's voice bellows from down the hall.

Soon after we see the man, and it's clearly the property owner.

"I need to see the man who is staying with you," I say.

"Man? I have no man staying here," he says. "Only my servants are here, and they're all women."

I look around and see what he's talking about. Boy, he has a lot of maids. Most of them are young girls, and it makes me wonder what's going on here.

We do a thorough search of the house and come up empty handed, so we're just about to leave, though I vow to check into this home-owner and find out why all these young girls are here. I mind-link James to have him get started on that right away.

I sigh. All these bad leads are getting me frustrated and angry.

"Hey, you."

I turn at the sound of Tristan's voice and notice a short, odd looking maid who's trying to walk quickly down the hall. There's a strange waddle to the maid's step, and I hitch up an eyebrow.

In my best Alpha voice, I call out, "Hey, you. Get back here!"

CHAPTER 39: NO ONE TAKES MY THRONE!

GENE

"Hey, you, Get back here!"

I freeze in my tracks, hearing Alpha Red-Headed Guy shout at me to stop. I am the Alpha King. He is nothing but a ginger peon. Yet, I find myself unable to take another step.

I don't understand this. His Alpha voice shouldn't have any effect on me whatsoever. Could it be that I'm just scared?

Of course not! I'm Alpha Gene! My mommy didn't raise me to be scared of anything.

Still, as I hear the heavy footsteps of Alpha Red-Headed Guy approaching me, I swallow hard. Why can't I remember anyone's name anymore? Maybe if I could use his name and command him, he'd have to leave me alone. But it's been a few weeks since I saw these guys, and the only names I can remember are Mary and Reba. Wait– those are girls' names. The Alphas have girl names?

"You, turn around and look at me," Alpha Red-Headed Guy demands.

"Me?" I say in a high-pitched voice. "Oh, I'm just a little old lady maid, sir. I'm no one."

"Do what Alpha Eli says." That's Alpha Curly-Haired Guy. I'd recognize his voice anywhere. It booms across the room, making my bones shake.

Slowly, I turn and look at Alpha Eli–the one with the bright red hair. I keep my own long black hair over my face. This wig is very flattering. When I caught my reflection in the mirror earlier, I couldn't help but think about how nice it would be to feed myself grapes.

A big grin breaks out across Alpha Elliott's face. "Well, well. If it isn't exactly who we are looking for." Turning to the older man standing across the room, the one who owns this house, I think, he asks, "Did you know he was here?"

"I… I…" he stammers. Alpha Sandy? Is that his name? Is that a boy name or a girl name?

"You what?" That's Alpha Mary. I turn to look at him, fluttering my eyelashes, hoping he might also think I'm lovely enough to feed him grapes.

"Yes, I knew he was here." The Alpha who owns the house hangs his head. "He's just a harmless old man."

"That harmless old man tried to kill your queen!" Alpha Curly Haired Guy barks. "He would've killed her with your next king still in her womb."

"Oh, fiddle faddle!" I declare. "I'm just a harmless old man."

Alpha Eleanor turns and looks at me. "I thought you were just a little old lady." He pulls my long black wig off my head and throws it on the ground.

I feel exposed, but I stand up straight. "I am not. I am your king, King Gene! And I demand all of you to bow to me at once."

"Oh, no you don't," Alpha Reba says, coming over toward us with his arms folded across his chest. "You abdicated the throne. You are no longer the king."

"And until my son is old enough to rule, the four of us will be in charge of the kingdom," Alpha Mary says, looking at me like he'd like to snap my puny little neck.

"But that's not fair!" I shout, stomping my foot. "This is my kingdom! Mine! I took it fair and square!"

"By faking your parents' deaths and locking them up!" Alpha Elizabeth says.

"That's not true!" I bellow, but when I stop and think about it, I believe it actually is true. That does sound like the very thing I did. "Well, I mean… that was a long time ago. It's my kingdom now."

"Not for long." Alpha Mary pulls out a piece of paper from his back pocket. It's rolled up, but he unfurls it and sets it on a table. "You're going to sign this, and then this matter will be settled once and for all."

"Sign what?" I bark at him. "I'm not signing anything. Guards, arrest this man!" I point at Alpha Mary, but no one else moves. I remember then that we're not in my castle. "Alpha Sandy, send your guards to arrest this man."

Alpha Sandy lets out a long sigh and runs his hand down his face. "I've told you a hundred times, Gene. My name is Alpha Andy."

"Oh, that's right." Hmm. I usually at least get the first letter right. "Well, arrest him." I am still pointing at Mary. "And him! And him! And him!" I point at all of the Alphas. "Arrest all of them and take me to my castle."

"No." Alpha Alice crosses her hands across her chest. "I'm staying out of this. If these Alphas want to take you, so be it. I know how the contest was supposed to go, and if one of them had a male baby, then that will be the next Alpha King. I'm not getting on their bad side."

"Appalling!" I shout. "You scoundrel! You're nothing more than the asshole on a maggot! Alpha Alice, arrest yourself as well."

"Gene," Alpha Curly-Haired Guy says, sauntering over with a pen in his hand. "Just sign the fucking document and come with us like a good little boy, huh?"

"Little boy? I have feathered boas in my closet that are older than you!" I shout, spraying him with spittle.

He wipes his face. "Feathered boas? In your closet? You're kinkier than I am, and that's saying something. Sign it."

I stare at him, giving him the death eye, the sort of stare a kindergarten teacher can use from fifty feet away to put the fear of Goddess in any of her charges.

He doesn't budge.

I crane my neck and stare harder, really getting into it, peering at him like he's a speck forty-eight miles away and I am straining to see him.

"Gene? Are you okay?" Alpha Curly-Haired Guy asks. "You, uh, need to go to the bathroom or something?" I say nothing, only continue to give him my most meaningful, menacing look. He turns to Alpha Alice. "Does he wear adult diapers or something? We may have a mess on our hands. With four babies, we know how to change diapers, but I'm not changing his."

"I think he's trying to make you change your mind," Alpha Alice says quietly.

That's it. We're on the right track. I growl at him, low in my throat.

He tips his head to the side.

I growl lower, like a boat motor in deep water.

His head is now sideways as he stares at me.

I am a conundrum. An enigma. I am a puzzle, and he is puzzling over me.

My grow becomes a bark. I bare my teeth, gnashing them at him.

I can see he is scared now as his eyes widen and he runs his hand through his mop of curls.

"Okay," Alpha Mary says, snatching the pen from Alpha Curly-Haired Guy. "That's enough of that. Just write your name right here, and we won't kill you, okay?"

I perk up at the mention of dying. "Kill me? Since when was there talk of you killing me?"

"Well, we can't just let you continue to run around free, causing havoc and bringing mischief wherever you go," Alpha Eliza says.

I giggle and cover my mouth with my palm. "I am full of mischief, that's true."

"We won't kill you if you sign it." Alpha Mary taps the paper where I'm supposed to write my name.

I raise my pen, thinking not being dead is probably better than being dead, but then another thought crosses my mind. "Wait–are you putting me in prison?" I think of my poor father down in the dungeon, losing his mind, my mother locked in the tower, missing her Gene-Gene. I don't wanna be like them.

"Nope. Just sign." Alpha Mary taps again.

I stare at him for a moment, trying to decide if I can trust him, but then Alpha Elsbeth pokes me hard in the back, and I know I'm out of options. I write my name on the paper.

Alpha Mary snatches it away before I have a chance to even dot the I in my name. Thankfully, there is no I in my name.

"Good. Thank the Goddess that's all over," Alpha Reba says.

"What are you going to do with me?" I feel a ripple of fear wash through me as I realize I am no longer king and have no control over anything.

"Goddess!" Alpha Mary takes a big step backward.

I look down. Someone must've spilled a cup of stinky water because there's a puddle on the floor beneath my skirt.

"Don't you worry, stinky pants," Alpha Curly-Haired Guy says. "You'll find out soon enough. Besides, I think you'll like it. You're already dressed for it." He winks at me, and I gulp for air.

I'm dressed like a woman.

Is he gonna make me feed him grapes?

CHAPTER 40: PERFECTION

ROSE

I love spending time out in the garden, and now I'm doing it with four little bundles of joy. I've heard that expression so many times, but now that I'm a mother, I really understand just how much joy those little bundles can bring. And with all the fear of losing them that I've experienced over the past weeks, I'm even more grateful for these beautiful pups next to me.

Right now, they're divided between Kelly and Shelby, with Shelby holding the boys and Kelly holding the girls. I have to smile looking at Shelby's face. I just know that she's going to want to be a mom herself very soon. I know she and Adam can handle it, and I bet they've already been talking about it. I hope they're already trying for a baby.

Kelly has that same look in her eyes. I guess it's hard to hold back the motherly instinct when you're holding little ones. I'm positive that she'll find her mate soon and will be a wonderful mother herself.

'Hey, little flower.'

I hear Tristan's voice in the mind-link and smile wide. All four of them have told me that they've found Gene, and they'll be home soon, and I can't wait.

'Hey, handsome,' I say. 'Are you almost home?'

'Walking through the front gate now,' he says.

'We're in the east garden,' I tell him.

Shelby looks at me and smiles. "I think someone has heard from her Alphas. Are they home?"

I laugh. "Yes, they'll be here shortly." I turn to Kelly. "When is your team planning on leaving for the resort?"

"As soon as your Alphas are settled in," Kelly replies. "A group of shifters from the resort actually came here first. They wanted to get supplies and speak to the Alphas, so I'll leave when they're done."

"They probably want to be pack members," Shelby chimes in. "I'm sure it's fine with the Alphas."

Kelly nods. "They just insisted on asking out of respect. I haven't met them yet. Once we're through here, I'll head over and introduce myself."

She stands while still holding the girls with precision skill and gently sets each one into the adorable strollers we're walking them around in. Shelby does the same with the boys with a forlorn look in her eye, like she doesn't want to let go. Yes, she and Adam are definitely trying already, I think.

I catch the scent of my handsome Alphas before I see them, and my smile gets wider still. When they step into the garden, I run up and throw my arms around the first one I see, who happens to be Tristan. He greets me with a touch of his soft lips that's gentle at first then presses in firmer as we both open our mouths slightly. The feel of his tongue against mine makes me close my eyes and moan.

But then I hear a throat clearing, breaking the moment.

I giggle against Tristan's lips as we part. Adam is looking at us with mock disapproval, and my giggle turns into a laugh.

"My mate and I will be watching your little ones for a while," Adam says.

Shelby smiles and takes one of the double strollers without another word, but she does give me a wink as she and Adam walk by.

I already miss my pups, but I haven't properly greeted my other Alphas yet, and we don't waste any time. First Mark, then Reece, then

Eli…. With each kiss, I feel like freezing time so I can enjoy the feel of them.

But apparently, they have something to talk to me about. I can tell by the look in their eyes. I look suspiciously at all three of them, and they all have smiles on their faces, so it can't be bad news, I assume.

Mark begins explaining first. "So, we've told you in the mind-link that we've found Gene."

I nod. Just the mention of that horrible man makes me wish we can just go back to kissing and stop talking, but I suppose I need to know what they've done to him. I hope it's at least as good as what I did to Barbara.

"We've brought him back to the castle," Mark says.

"You've what?" Just the idea of that monster near my babies gets my blood boiling already.

"It's okay, darlin'," Reece chimes in. "He'll never be anywhere near you. We have… plans for him."

Tristan starts laughing, and I look at him like he's lost his mind. Maybe he has. They have plans for Gene here in Mark's castle?

"He's going to be a maid here, with special duties… poopy duties," Tristan explains with another laugh.

"What?" I ask.

Eli shakes his head. "Personally, I wanted to hang the bastard, but we reached a consensus. We're not going to take our eyes off him, and he's going to clean all the diapers in the castle. We might even have him expand to the whole kingdom if he acts up."

"You're letting him near our pups?" I can't believe my Alphas are even considering such a thing.

"No, little flower," says Tristan.

The smile on his face and twinkle in his eye made my heart skip a beat.

"He's not allowed anywhere near our precious little pups," he clarifies. "Just the diapers. Dirty diapers, all day long… that's his new job! We'll watch him every second."

"But you don't have time to watch Gene clean diapers," I say.

"Nope, we have a new employee for that," says Reece. "This guy won't take his eyes off him. Well, of course he'll get breaks. When he's sleeping or needs time off, the guards will watch Gene."

I shake my head. "What guy?"

"Eustace!" says Tristan. That gleam is still in his eye. It makes me want to wrap my arms around him.

"Eustace agreed to that?" I ask.

"Yep, and he's excited about it," says Tristan. "We created a full-time job for him with lots of good benefits, and he's looking forward to living in the castle. We gave him a full suite to enjoy. He's got one of the most important jobs in the castle."

I look at all my Alphas, one by one, silently at first, then I burst out laughing. My Alphas join in, and I give them each a few more kisses.

"I think it's my night, isn't it?" asks Tristan after the laughter dies down.

I look at him and melt in his suggestive gaze. It's about time I gave my Alphas some special attention. We all deserve it.

He takes me in his arms and our lips meet again, my eyes closing and my tongue dancing against his. I feel three hands, one after the other, touching the small of my back as my other Alphas wish me a goodnight and leave the garden. Once alone, Tristan lifts me up and spins me around, both of us laughing as he practically runs with me down the hall to my room.

We don't say a word as he lays me down gently on the bed and steps back to go lock the door. I instantly feel the loss of his touch, but it only lasts a moment before he's back with me again in bed.

"The babies," I manage to say between kisses.

He stops and pulls back from me, and I get to look into those beautiful eyes of his again, and this time, they're heavy with want.

I shake my head. "I mean I have a few hours before the babies need me again."

A growl escapes his lips. "Then I'm going to make the most of it."

We make short work of our clothes, each of us peeling off the other's in a desperate need to remove any hint of distance between us. I think absently about how nights with Tristan usually involve toys or some sort of wild position, but we don't have time for that.

We need each other, now.

He lays me back again and traces his finger down the side of my face and continues down my neck, not stopping until he reaches my left breast and wraps his full hand around it. I moan at the sensation, but he doesn't stop there. His hand moves gently down the curve of my waist and toward my belly, then lowers slowly. I already feel moisture building between my legs.

"Want," is the only word I can say, and Tristan smirks and traces his fingers around my hot, wet folds.

"Oh, you'll get everything you want, little flower," he says in a gravelly whisper.

That about sends me over the edge right now, and we've barely started. He's as anxious for it as I am. We'll go slow some other time. In a moment, he's on top of me, his rock-hard cock rubbing against my folds.

But then he pauses.

"Are you sure you're all right with this, little flower?" he says softly.

I nod, nearly frantically. The healers have given me the all-clear long ago. The birth of my four pups had been rough on me, but I've healed quickly.

I'm more than ready for this.

That's all the go-ahead Tristan needs as he slides inside me. I gasp a little as I have to adjust for his size, but my wetness compensates for some of that. It's only a brief moment before we were in a comfortable rhythm.

And then it goes far beyond comfort.

With every stroke he hits the perfect spot, my moans only quieted by our lips pressing desperately together. I'm at my edge in what feels like seconds, and I try to hold back a little to savor the moment and make it last.

"Let it go, little flower," he moans.

That's all I need to go over the edge. Within seconds of my walls squeezing tightly against his stiff cock, he lets loose himself. We cry out together, and my vision blurs from the pleasure of it.

He collapses against me gently then rolls over and pulls me into his chest, his arms never letting go. It takes a while to catch my breath, and when I look up into his eyes, he's smiling at me with every inch of his handsome face.

I trace his chiseled arm muscle with my finger and sigh.

Life is perfect.

CHAPTER 41: A WONDERFUL LIFE

MARK

It's my turn to spend the night with Rose, and I can hardly wait. It is a little odd being in this position, sharing my mate with four other men, but now that we have our situation settled, I realize I wouldn't want it any other way.

I'm carrying flowers as I go into her room. I think she's probably in bed, resting, after another long day of caring for the babies.

Instead, I find her in the bathtub–naked and bubbly–and I grin at her.

"Well, hello there, Alpha Mark," she says from the large tub filled with warm, sudsy water. "Care to join me?"

I lay the flowers on the counter and quickly strip, a big grin on my face. She watches me, and I think maybe it would be sexier if I slowed down, but I can hardly breathe watching her run her hand over her bare arm, washing herself with the foam from the bubbles.

Soon enough, I'm naked and in the tub with her. I scoot behind her, holding her, and pick up a bar of soap and a washcloth.

I take my time washing her even though she already smells like flowers and couldn't possibly be dirty–except for, hopefully, her thoughts.

When I get to her folds, she begins to moan. I take my time, washing her carefully, and then drop the cloth and use my fingers, pushing inside of her, caressing her most sensitive area with my thumb.

Without warning, Rose swirls around in the tub, sending a splash of water onto the floor. She straddles me, taking my dick in her hand, and slowly gliding down until she's consumed me. I close my eyes, relishing the feel of her on my body.

She begins to move up and down, slowly at first, creating little splashes of water, and then she moves faster until both of us are grunting and panting. I kiss her deeply, my hands resting on her perfect hips. When we come, it's together.

I open my eyes, feeling a little stunned. Even though we've been together for a while now, that never gets old. "Goddess, I love you," I murmur.

"I love you, too." She kisses me lightly and then asks, "Wanna go again?"

I chuckle and say, "Always." My dick is already hard again, and we get back to it.

Even though I'm sharing my sweet Rose with three other men, I was her first, and that's something no one can ever take away from us.

~

Rose

IT'S SO nice having all four of my men back in the castle. They are busy doing Alpha stuff, but I still see them a lot more now that there are now wars.

That also means we will be relocating soon. There's no point in us staying here when Dark Forest is empty. Soon, we'll need to go back.

I try not to think about that as I do one last check on the babies. Once I've kissed them goodnight and I'm assured that Shelby will be watching over them all night, along with their nurses that I trust, I head to my room.

I've just slipped into a short, red nightgown when there's a knock at the door. I'd recognize that knock anywhere. "Come in, Reece."

He's grinning when he steps through the door. "Hello, my beautiful queen."

"Hello, my handsome Alpha." I'm excited to see him. It's been too long since the two of us have been together–something like three days. That's too long.

Reece glides in and kisses me, his hand going right to my breast. "This is a nice outfit," he says. "But it would look nicer on the floor."

I giggle and start unbuttoning his shirt while he continues to fondle my breasts through the thin silk. I make him stop long enough to slip his hands out of his shirt, but then, his mouth comes down on a nipple. He takes it between his lips and sucks, licking at the same time, and I forget how to unzip and can't get his pants off.

After a moment, I remember and quickly free him from the rest of his clothes. He pulls my nightgown over my head and tosses it exactly where he thought it should go and then lays me on the bed,

All I'm wearing now is a tiny red thong. He stands at the foot of the bed and takes me in. "Damn," he murmurs, and I smile up at him, dragging a hand down my middle.

"Come on," I breathe, and he leaps onto the bed, bouncing me up into the air. I laugh until his mouth covers mine. Then, he breaks one side of the thong with his hands and then the other, and I'm bared to him.

Reece slips his fingers along my slit. My head rocks back. He's testing to see if I'm ready–and I most definitely am. Feeling that for himself, he pushes my legs open and positions himself between them. I grab hold of him and pull him to me. His entire length slides inside of me.

He begins to move, and I rock my hips to meet his, my mouth open in a silent scream of pleasure. Reece kisses the side of my face by my ear and then kisses a trail down before finding my mouth again with his.

He takes his time, making each movement count, and before long, I am tumbling over the edge. Soon enough, he joins me, and then we are both panting, writhing, groaning together until we collapse on the bed.

"Goddess, you're so amazing, Rose," he whispers, reaching over to pull me toward him. "I love you so much."

"I love you, too." My heart hammers in my chest. I can't really breathe yet, but I know that what I'm saying is true. I love him so much, I can hardly stand that. I feel the same way about all my men.

Reece moves us so that we are beneath the blanket. I rest my head on his muscular bicep and stare up into his eyes. I think of the first time I saw him and how I thought he was so handsome, I could hardly comprehend it. I'm so lucky to have four amazing men to call my own, but each of them is different, and I've always admired how level-headed Reece is.

"What are you thinking about?" he asks, smiling down at me as he caresses my cheek with his thumb.

"Just how amazing this life we have is. That's all." I say it like it's simple, but it's not. We've all overcome a great deal to get here. I'm sure we'll have challenges in our future, but I'm confident we'll over-come them, too.

"When Gene first asked me to participate in this, I didn't want to," he admits. "I thought it sounded silly. And I didn't really think I wanted to be the Alpha King or have a child of mine be the Alpha King. But then I thought about my pack and my family, my ancestors, and I wanted our legacy to be something great. Now, I have a beautiful mate, a beautiful daughter, and my pack is so proud of everything I've done. You're right, my beautiful queen. This is a pretty damn good life we have."

I am still grinning when he leans down to kiss me. I've often wondered what the Alphas' motivation was to join the contest. I assume they all have similar reasons. None of them are greedy or power hungry, but they are all proud of their packs and their ancestry. I bet all of them would say the same thing.

Reece stops kissing me just in time as I stifle a yawn. I close my eyes, loving the feeling of his arms around me. If this is what I have to look forward to for the rest of my life, I am going to be one happy woman.

Forever.

CHAPTER 42: CLOSE ENOUGH

Rose

I can't believe how much the Goddess has blessed me. I remember all the times I was hunched over on the floor of the sewage plant trying to force myself to breathe through my mouth to avoid the stench. It didn't work very well. I also remember all those lonely nights in my high school years when I was exhausted from working and barely had time to do half my homework, knowing I'd be punished by my parents for falling behind.

I would look up at the moon and beg the Goddess to make my life better.

Now I have four beautiful children and four handsome and kind Alphas who all love me, not to mention my wonderful friends and all the caring people in Mark's castle who are so nice to me. Had I known this was my future, I would have scrubbed those floors with a wide smile on my face.

We're now in the courtyard of the beautiful castle, and I'm about to say goodbye to one of those dear friends. But it's not a sad time. Kelly is going to do wonderful things for those people who have been living in that abandoned resort and are in such desperate need of help.

She's certainly well-equipped. The whole courtyard is full of a huge caravan of people and equipment ready to fix up the resort.

Eustace is all smiles. "Remember that Eleanor needs somethin' to do," he says. "She don't get around much anymore, but she's a real wiz at the knittin' and stuff."

Kelly smiles back at him. "Don't worry. We'll give everyone something to do that suits their capabilities. She'll be a welcome member of the pack."

Since Eli and Kelly are the ones who discovered the place—or maybe it's more accurate to say that the place discovered them—the Alphas have agreed that the entire grounds of the resort will belong to Eli's pack. He's agreed to make official pack members of anyone who wants in, and those who want to be independent can still stay there peacefully. I love how my Alphas care so much about people.

I wrap my arms around my friend and feel a few tears welling in my eyes. "I'm going to miss you."

We pull back and Kelly shakes her head. "I won't be gone long. Yes, it'll take a while to rebuild the place, but I'll be back for breaks. I don't want to be away from my sweet little nephew very long."

"Well, I'm so proud of you," I say. "This is such a wonderful thing you're doing for these people."

"They're good people, so it's a pleasure to help them," she says. "I met a few of the people who came to talk to the Alphas last night. The rest were going to meet us out here this morning. They must be around here somewhere."

She looks around and her brow furrows slightly.

"What's wrong?" I ask.

"I don't know," she says. "I just feel funny. It's strange."

I feel a warm, strong hand on the small of my back, and I smile. Eli's scent fills my nostrils.

Yep, I'm a long way from the floors of the sewage plant.

"You'd better be careful on your trip," Eli says firmly to Kelly.

She rolls her eyes. "You do remember that I'm the one who went off to rescue you, right?"

He laughs, and when he does, he pulls me closer against his warm

214

body. Tonight is Eli's night with me, and I can't wait. I can tell that he's excited for it, too.

"Yeah, yeah," he says. "Just watch your back out there."

"Always the big brother," she complained. "When are you going to realize that with my warrior training, I—"

She pauses mid-sentence, and her eyes are wide and sparkly looking. It's like her whole face is glowing. I look at Eli and he shrugs, but then I trace Kelly's gaze and find the source of her current state.

He's a handsome man, tall and muscular with bright blond hair, and he's looking at Kelly the same way she's looking at him.

"Mate," she whispers, almost inaudibly, but I'm close enough to hear it.

I gasp and step back, taking Eli with me and leaving them some room to come together. I can't get the grin off my face as I watch the Moon Goddess's magic right unfold in front of my eyes. I turn to Eli, and he's lowered his brows a tad, and I have to laugh. While Kelly and her mate join in a kiss, I turn Eli's head so we can do the same.

"He's her mate," I whisper in his ear after tasting his delicious lips. "He'll take care of her."

Eli seems only half-convinced, and once Kelly and this guy are finally separated, he clears his throat.

"I'm going to need the name of the guy who just sucked face with my sister," he says firmly. "And I need to know where you're from, and whether you have a criminal record, and—"

Kelly slaps Eli's shoulder, and that quiets him instantly, and I'm laughing so hard I've just about let loose those tears I was forming a moment ago when saying goodbye to her.

The man gave Eli the sign of respect. "Alpha King Eli, my apologies for not paying the proper respects before," he says. "I'm Corbin. I came across the rogues at the resort about a week ago. They're good people, and I'd like to see them restore the place and have a good life."

"You seem to be an Alpha," Eli says. "What pack are you from?"

Corbin shakes his head. "I'm of no pack. I don't know about being an Alpha because I have no idea who my father is. My mother and I lived from place to place. Since she passed, I've just been on my own, doing odd jobs for a living here and there."

"Well, it appears you're in Beach pack now," says Eli, holding out his hand.

Corbin takes it and shakes it firmly. "Thank you, sir."

Eli shakes his head. "Call me Eli. And this is our beautiful Queen Rose."

A warm smile passes over Corbin's face as he bows to me.

I giggle. "Please call me Rose."

I hold onto Eli as we wave goodbye, and the entourage pours out of the courtyard with Corbin's arm held firmly around Kelly.

AFTER A WONDERFUL DAY with my Alphas and our pups, it was time for my night with Eli.

There's a different feeling in our kisses than I've had with my other Alphas. Yes, I feel the same need in me to feel him inside, but there's something else.

I just need to feel him close to me. I suppose it's from the time he was missing, but I just can't pull him close enough to satisfy this need.

"What's wrong, baby?" he whispers between kisses.

So, he notices it, too.

"I don't know," I say. "I just... I guess it's because of all that fear I had when you were missing."

He pulls back from the kisses and rolls onto his back, pulling me onto his chest.

"Our babies were gone, you were gone... it's just... I guess I never let out all the pain from that," I say.

"It's okay, baby," he says, squeezing me tight. "These last few weeks have been really rough on you. You finally have some time to let all that out."

"I don't want to spoil our night—"

"You could never spoil a night we have together," he says quickly.

"Just being with you is enough. We have plenty of time. Just let it happen, baby."

With that, tears stream down my cheeks, and he reaches up his hand to tenderly wipe them away. But he doesn't try to make me stop. He just lets me cry out all the frustration I've been feeling. He strokes my back with his strong hands all the while.

"We're back," he says. "We're safe. You never need to be away from the pups again. And Rose—" He pulls my chin up gently with his fingers so I'm looking into his eyes. "My beautiful queen, I promise I'll never be apart from you again."

He pulls me in for a kiss, and his lips taste so good, his tongue feels just right against mine. I moan into his mouth as he gently rearranges us so he's on top of me. He sweeps back my hair so it's out of my face and gazes at me. I see nothing but love in his eyes.

His lips are on mine again in the next moment, and I close my eyes, savoring his taste once again. I feel him gently spread my legs apart as his fingers work their way to my folds.

He explores outside for a moment but then moves one of them in, then two, preparing my entrance for his rock-hard cock.

I'm about ready to come even before he's inside me, and thankfully he doesn't waste a second. In the next moment, he's in me with firm, purposeful strokes that hit every spot just right.

"Eli," I cry out.

I'm not going to last much longer. I don't hold back, and don't think I could if I tried, as one more scream comes out of my throat, and his voice seems to echo as he hollers my name.

Finally, Eli is close enough to me.

CHAPTER 43: EPILOGUE

Rose

It feels strange going back to Castle Dark Forest, and it's going to feel even weirder being there again. It's been so long since I first arrived there for the stupid contest... well, I guess without that contest, I would have never met my Alphas, so I suppose I won't call it stupid anymore.

I wouldn't mind staying in Mark's castle forever... or Tristan's, or Eli's, or Reece's, and I tell my Alphas as much, but they all assure me we'll visit all of them often. The kingdom is used to having Castle Dark Forest be the home of the Alpha King, and I agree that it's probably best that we live there.

Still... it's going to be odd being there, remembering King Gene trying to kill me, among other things that happened there.

"Are you okay, little flower?" Tristan reaches out his hand and wraps it around my fingers. The calming feel of him instantly washes away my fears.

"It's okay to be nervous about coming here," says Reece, who is sitting across from me in the vehicle. It's sort of a cross between a van and an SUV, and the back seats face each other. "If you find yourself too uncomfortable here, we'll leave."

I shake my head. "I'm okay, especially since we left Gene behind."

I am relieved about that. Eustace really liked Mark's castle and the suite he was in, so he asked to stay there. It turns out there are plenty of pups living there and in the surrounding area, so Gene will keep being a poopy diaper maid far away from my little ones.

And that's fine by me.

We pass through the gates, and I'm relieved to find that I'm not feeling nervous at all. Things feel different now. I'm the queen of this kingdom now, and my four Alphas are Alpha Kings, and my little ones are two princesses and two princes, one of which is heir to the throne. It's a lot different than being brought here in a train full of young women ready to pull my hair out because they want to eliminate the competition to have an Alpha's baby.

And it's a hell of a long way from any sewage plant.

I'm certainly greeted differently, with servants everywhere making way as we all get out of the vehicle to carry all the babies inside.

I step out, turn around, and see for the first time what a huge entourage we've brought with us. Most of these cars are full of warriors who fought in the war, and they're finally returning home. The courtyard is full of women and children running toward their mates to welcome them. It's making for an amazing scene.

Adam and Shelby step out of the castle and walk over. They'd left yesterday so they could get here before the rest of us. The first thing Shelby does is hold up her arms so she can hold one of the babies. I smile and hand over Reeva, who I happen to be holding.

But Shelby looks different, and I can't really place it. She looks... super happy. She's always happy, but this is different. I'm just about to say something when Adam speaks up, talking to my Alphas.

"I'll understand if you need us to vacate the Beta quarters," he says.

"What?!" I ask. "Why?

"Well, all the Alpha Kings have their own Betas, so the Beta position is more than filled," Adam says.

I look at my Alphas with a desperate plea in my eyes. I don't want Shelby to leave.

Tristan is the first to speak. "Did you seriously think that? Come on, man. Are you kidding me?"

Adam looks confused.

Mark shakes his head. "There's no way we're letting you retire that easily," he says, in a bit of a teasing tone.

"I'm sorry we didn't speak to you earlier," says Reece. "We didn't know you felt that way. We need you here."

Adam's face starts to brighten up as Eli chimes in. "You know this place like the back of your hand. You know everyone who does business with this castle and this kingdom. You have relationships with all the vendors, and you've been running this place for years while that idiot Gene was neglecting his duties."

Mark nods. "We were hoping that you'd stay and be Chief Advisor Beta to the Alpha Kings," he says.

Adam's eyes go wide. "Is that... do you... I mean, is that even a thing?"

"It is now, buddy," says Tristan. "But it's a mouthful. Maybe we'll just call you the Chief Beta."

He puts up his hand and messes up Adam's hair, and we all start laughing.

I smile at Shelby, feeling so happy that she's going to stay here. I know that Kelly needs to be with her mate, so I'm dealing with that, but I don't want Shelby to move away, too.

But she has a funny look on her face. "Well, but—"

Adam walks over to her and wraps his arm around her shoulders. They look at each other with wide smiles.

"Um... we might need to move out of that suite after all," he says.

I look at Shelby. "Shelby... why?"

She looks like she's about to burst, and she finally spits it out. "Because I'm pregnant!"

My eyes go wide, and I want to grab her and jump up and down, but I don't want to squish Reeva, so I do a milder equivalent of that, which involves one arm and bouncing more than jumping. I can't get the smile off my face. "I'm so happy for you two!"

"Congratulations, Chief Beta," says Mark. He shakes Adam's hand, and the others follow suit.

"If you need more space, we can knock out some walls, or we can find you another suite," says Reece. "I think I remember seeing some good rooms on the east side that looked vacant."

"We've filled one suite on the east side," says Adam. "Retired Alpha King Edward and Former Queen Marcella are residing there."

"Oh," says Eli. "How are they doing?"

"They're much better than before," Adam says. "They're together. Edward has his wits about him now that he's not locked away in a prison without his mate. He's all-in on you four being Alpha Kings until the boy is ready to take over. His wife still has some issues, but her mental health is improving now that she's with her mate as well."

"That's good to hear," I say. "I'll have to go visit her. She's the only former queen I know. Maybe she can help me with a few things."

"Good idea, little flower," says Tristan.

"We'd better get these little ones inside and settled," says Mark. "Queen Rose, please lead the way!"

"With pleasure!" I say.

~

SEVEN MONTHS LATER...

I STEP out of the room where I just put down the tiniest bundle of joy in the castle—Shelby and Adam's little newborn boy. It's been tough being on the assistant side of a birth, and I'm exhausted. It only makes me appreciate all the nurses and everyone else who helped with my quadruple birth even more than I did before.

I stroll into our giant Alpha King suite, which is big enough to have separate rooms for me, all my Alphas, and all our little pups. I'm greeted by all four of my Alphas in the living room area, each one with their respective son or daughter.

The children look so big. We've been planning for a major first birthday party in a couple of months, but I put that on hold when Shelby went into labor. I have a lot of help, so I'm sure we'll be ready regardless.

I had wanted to collapse into my bed before I walked through the door, but now I'm energized. All four of my pups are in different stages of walking, crawling, pulling themselves up on everything, or just scooting along. I'm not rushing anyone. They'll all develop at their own pace.

The most energetic one is Tristan's little Trisha, who just might be capable of running the kingdom on her own one day. She's still so little, but I can imagine her talking her brothers into letting her rule the kingdom before either of them step up to the throne. The idea makes me smile.

To think that she was the last one missing and the hardest to find... I put that idea out of my head. That's all in the past now. Today, we're all together and have a bright future.

I can tell my Alphas were discussing kingdom business, which is almost a constant subject now. They run ideas by me all the time. I love how they want me to take a leading role in running the kingdom as well.

"We need your input," Mark always says. "Half of these wars and conflicts wouldn't happen in the first place if the Queen had gone into the issue first with compassion and negotiating skills. We want life to be fair for everyone in our kingdom, and you're an important part of that."

My cheeks go warm at the thought.

I sit with my Alphas, and we play with the babies as we discuss the latest issues troubling the kingdom, after I report on Shelby and Adam and their little pup, of course. They've named him Aiden, and he's just adorable.

As we're chatting, I think about everything that's led me to this place, these wonderful Alphas, and these beautiful children. It's been a long journey full of so much heartache and pain, but the love I have now is worth every second of suffering.

Every one of my Alphas is a kind, generous, caring man who is also brave, strong, and driven by high morals. Alone they could lead any kingdom, but together, they are going to make this a place where families can thrive.

Every one of my babies is precious and beautiful, and their individual personalities shine through so much that I am confident for all their futures.

"Are you okay, darlin'?" asks Reece.

"I'm perfect," I say.

A lone tear has formed in the corner of my eye, but it's not for sadness at all. I'm just overflowing with gratitude to the Moon Goddess for giving me such a beautiful life as Queen with my four Alpha Kings.

THE END

CONTINUE the story in *Descendants of the Breeder!*

ALSO BY BELLA MOONDRAGON

One Night with the Billionaire

Shared by the Sexy Billionaire Twins

The Alpha King's Breeder series:

Bought by the Alpha: The Alpha King's Breeder Book 1

Loved by the Alpha: The Alpha King's Breeder Book 2

Lost by the Alpha: The Alpha King's Breeder Book 3

Luna of the Alpha: The Alpha King's Breeder Book 4

Legacy of the Alpha: The Alpha Kings's Breeder Book 5

Daughter of the Alpha: The Alpha King's Breeder Book 6

Descendants of the Alpha: The Alpha King's Breeder Book 7

Shadow of the Alpha: The Alpha King's Breeder Book 8

The Luna's Vampire Prince series:

The Culling

The Kingdom

The Conquered

Pregnant With Four Alphas' Babies

Chosen As the Breeder

Mated to Four Alphas

Threats Against the Breeder

At War for the Breeder

The Stolen Breeder

Four Alphas, Four Babies

Becoming the Luna Queen

Descendants of the Breeder (releases 9/1/2024)

Desired by the Devil series

Whispers of the Devil

Bantor of the Devil (coming soon)

The Mafia Kings series

Indebted to the Mafia King

Sign up for Bella's newsletter here.

Follow Bella on Facebook here.